Showdown

The tall one, he didn't expect this. Not from a stranger half-breed in town, wearing a marshal's badge. It rankled him and the fury in his eyes showed it.

I began counting, knowing it might be my final breath. No matter. I had a job to do … and I'd opened the ball.

"Three … four …"

I counted slow and easy, so as the town could hear me.

He just stood there looking me over, unsure of where I'd been … and who I was. When I got to *seven*, his hand swept down for iron.

Enjoy more great titles by P K Brown:

The Llano Kid

Dead Man's Gold

Double Cross

Aqualene

The Llano Kid

Cactus Valley Lawman

Book 3   Copyright 2019

Riding Point

A day's hard ride west into the Mojave Desert took me well past sundown when I hooked up with a small wagon train traveling west to Los Angeles. The roan, weary from the miles, paused near the outline of scrubby manzanita outside their camp.

"I'm friendly. Can I come in?"

The light of their fire lit up wary faces. "Alright … Walk in slow with your hands where we can see 'em." The voice came from a bearded man back in the shadows. He held a large caliber rifle. I left Smoke to graze on scrub grass and stood in the fires light.

"Smelled your campfire a mile or two back," I said. "Don't run into many folks in the open desert."

"Well, light and set," one of the men replied friendly like. "Billy, take that man this here plate. I'll get the coffee."

I smiled at the lad, gazing at the food he handed me. "Beats cowboy rations. Been some time since I ate a woman-cooked meal."

We talked a mite about their trip west, the desert heat, water sources, dust storms, and the like. This was my first crossing so I was looking for whatever I could learn from these folks, but I gained little. Finally one of the fellas, he just laid it out straight.

"We be needin' a man with trail savvy who can read sign and keep his ear to the ground." He was a tall rangy man with cobalt eyes who went by Tom McCann. "Had us a site of trouble back yonder with a nasty band of Utes. Then a couple of run-ins with renegading Mexicans rustling our stock at night. Can't afford to lose any we still got. And I figure you might know how to use them fancy shootin' irons you're wearing... So how about it, young man?"

Well, I'd barely time to ask for seconds and gulp down the tin cup of coffee I was holding when they throwed that question at me.

"Reckon I could use the meals ... if they's all this good," My eyes met his. "And did you mention wages?"

"Yep, we'll pay you by the day!" That was a man in a fancy vest and smoking a cigar talking.

"You gotta name?" says the man still holdin' that Sharps repeater across his lap since I rode into camp.

"They call me the Kid. The Llano Kid," I replied, devouring what was still on my plate.

Now I just set there at that fire a mopping that tin clean whilst the men over yonder was a lookin' me over, and fussin' out the details in stealthy whispers. Suddenly they stopped and McCann stood up.

"Alright, fella, you got a deal," he said, and he starts pullin' money out of a leather satchel. "We'll front you wages, but one day at time."

Thinking on it right quick, a feller just ain't got much reason to turn down a deal like that.

We pulled out early the next morning.

The entire band was no more than twenty-five, thirty people when you count the young-uns I seen huddled around the fire eyeing my bronze colored face and coal-black hair dangling down under my hat. They could see I was of Injun blood, mixed with something white, but I'd been friendly enough at their campfire.

Now their daddies was hiring me almost sight unseen after the guide they'd recruited fell ill back at the Colorado River crossing.

I rode point all day and with the help of a little horse sense, tracked down a sizeable water hole near an outcrop of boulders below a jagged ridge. We took little time to eat lunch and I was out ahead of the wagons in the blazing heat, watching our back trail when I could find a high point. From the crest of a hill about twelve miles later I searched the plains to the north, looking for any movement or wisps of dust climbing into the copper sky. By sundown we had the stock bedded down, but a few horses still cropping dried scrub grass.

I sat with my feet up at the fire, taking in the sounds of darkness. The women had stowed the dishes and put the children to bed when McCann walked up.

"Got you on the early-mornin' watch. So get some shut-eye and Fred will come for yuh around two."

I nodded, pocketed the three-dollars in cash money he handed me and stretched out under my blanket atop some pine-needles yonder from the fire. I could hear my stubborn but loyal roan a-grazing near the small crick we was camped on, maybe twenty-feet off the trail. By now the others had turned in, except for Fred on first watch.

I must have been asleep two or three hours. Suddenly my eyes opened. T'was past midnight, by the position of the stars. A sound reached my ears … from behind some prickly pear. The roan had his head up and his ears pricked forward. Something was out there, aside from Fred who'd been watchin' camp from cover on a ridge yonder.

I lay right still. Sniffing a gentle breeze that rolled past, my ears keenly took in the sounds. Creatures of the night were about. A snake slithered by. A coon washed his hands down at the water's edge. Then the silhouette of a young boy appeared from behind a dwarf pine.

When he seen me sittin' up lookin' straight at him, he nearly jumped out of this skin.

"Hello, young feller," I offered in a soft whisper. "Out for a toilet stop?"

It was Billy. He nodded shyly and slinked over to me. I glanced about, still checking the midnight air. He just come right out with it.

"What kinda Injun are you, Mister Llano?"

I smiled at his curious innocence. "Reckon you never heard of the Cherokee, being this far west."

"Cher-o-kee." He slowly recited the word back to me. "Ya, I heard of 'em. How come you didn't try to kill us?"

At that I chuckled. "Not all us Indians are trouble, young fella. Most just want to be left alone … peacefully on our land."

He took that in and held it. "Is Llano a Injun name?"

"No, Billy. That was a name I—
You sure you want to hear about that, at this hour?"

"Is it bad?"

"Well. Uh. No!" I hesitated, not wanting to get into my past, fearing the boy would surely get the wrong idea about guns and fighting and such. But he stood there patiently, and I was never good at hiding the truth from honest folks.

"Yuh see, Billy, after I left Tennessee behind me, my horse and I ended up in south Texas where I lived in a small village settled mostly by Mexicans. The place was called Llano. I got on okay as a fourteen-year-old orphan, but one day I ran into trouble with a couple of ornery vaqueros, they're like wranglers. Anyway, them two wanted to give me a whipping."

"Why?"

"Cuz I was a misfit boy. Had no parents … and I was a half-breed. So, I fought back, and a well-placed left hook laid one of 'em out cold. His partner thought I'd killed him and drew his gun on me. Suddenly it was me or him … so I shot the pistol out of his hand. Then he drew his other gun, and my second shot put a hole through his hand.

"Folks in the village started talking. Claimed I could have shot him dead, fair and square. Said I was a bigger man to avoid a killing. Rumors got around that Llano had a kid with a mighty fast gun. Next thing I know they was callin' me the *Llano Kid*."

Billy looked at me in the moonlight. "So, what's your real name?"

"*Atsila*. My Cherokee name I use among my people. Means fire. I was born when the whites were burning some of us out, whilst we was hiding back in the Tennessee hills. My mother was Cherokee. My pa was Irish. Both are dead."

"So, that makes you a half-breed?"

"Yep. And that's all some folks call me. But you can call me Llano." I caught him yawning through a boyish smile. "Now you git back to bed b'fore your ma finds you missing."

Billy told me about losing his pa to cholera, then sauntered away in the moonlight, and crept back into the wagon. I slid back into bed and dosed.

Fred never got within ten yards of me before I was sitting up and reading the early morning air. He waved a hand and turned on his heel for his bedroll.

I checked my loads and slipped on my moccasins, then set out to circling the camp. Smoke rolled his eyes at me and went back to cropping scrub grass. My watch duty gave me a chance to count the wagons and livestock I'd be living with for the next couple weeks. Few of the families had been at the evening fire so I'd be meeting many more folks at daybreak.

The pre-dawn hours passed without incident. The moon dropped below the ridge. Sunrise painted the sky orange to the east whilst the last stars blinked out. The mules were just getting to their feet when some of the men in the group rode out to herd them down to the creek. A couple of fires were now burning and the smell of coffee drifted about the cool morning air.

The women folk set slabs of bacon to sizzling over the fire. Others were collecting eggs from hens that nested on the tail-boards of their wagons. On foot I helped move the livestock over to a fresh patch of ground, then waited for the men to migrate toward the grub line before joining them. Reckon I was a mite shy about showin' up for breakfast when a good bit of these folks had never laid eyes on me.

Suddenly I seen Tom McCann come over to make an announcement: "Gather round folks, Git yer breakfast and set." He handed me a plate and gestured at the table where the women folk were servin' grits, fried eggs, and hot bacon.

After he led off with a blessing, he cleared his throat, positioned betwixt the two fires. "Folks, we done some hirin' last night after some of you turned in. This here is Mister Llano. He's gonna be helpin' out with security matters, aside from scouting for water and safe spots to camp."

Folks was lookin' me up and down, some nodding their approval. Others were staring at my moccasin feet or my low hangin' pistols. Then some feller off to the side hollers: "That there is an Injun! We can't be trustin' no Injun to take us across the Mojave to Californee! And what about our women folk? Why they'd be—"

"Now hold up there, Frank! Don't be jumping the gun on me. I can vouch for Mister Llano. A 'fore gettin' yerself half-cocked, yuh need to hear me out!"

One of the women stepped back from the fire waving a spatula in her hand. "You pipe down, Frank. So quickly you forget ... that sidewinder you hired after we left the river, he done robbed us and took out with two of our best horses. And he was *white*!"

With all the hollering and fussin', it took several minutes for Tom McCann to bring order to the group.

"Now, it just so happens…" he says loud and clear. "I knew what we was buying us when I hired this young man. After all, he *is* the Llano Kid." Ole Tom, he let that sink into their skulls, figgering some might recognize the name.

His eyes sparkled. "A week ago when I come up that trail out of Prescott, I come upon a soldier who'd been in town a day or two earlier, about the time when they was gonna hang the Llano Kid. That was until a Ranger come to town and helped straighten the whole mess out. You see, Llano here is known down in Texas for lending a hand to the law when one is needed."

"Yah, I heard tell of him, too," said a man sitting on a boulder shakin' out his boots. "They say he's a mite handy with them guns, yet he ain't kilt nobody. Aims for the hand so the fella shootin' at him won't be gunnin' nobody for a good long time."

Well, I reckon them two kinda settled that, and I could see Tom McCann was relieved that Frank had backed off his remarks. Then Tom finished his business of introducing me while the children in the group come up to me with gaping mouths. Now, I don't cotton much to all that attention, so I tipped my hat to the ladies doin the cookin' and took up to hitching the livestock to the wagons.

We'd broke camp and put a good ten miles on that trail when I decided to scout on ahead a ways. And sure as a coon-raid in a hen-house, I seen the tracks of unshod horses crossin' our trail. They was fresh, after a brief rainstorm come down from the mountains north of us earlier that morning. The rough broken land surrounding me was already parched dry from a scorching noon sun. The air lay still and heavy.

Then I seen 'em coming. Over that ridge yonder, slanting off the trail and flattening out over the prairie. Six Utes on horses, painted for war! So I slid my Winchester out of its scabbard. Laying it across my thigh, I sat that roan and waited for 'em to pull up. Utes were abundant out here and some were stirred up by run-ins with the U.S. Cavalry. Apaches roamed here and there but were largely south and east of us.

Them Utes come toward me at a canter b'fore slowing their ponies to a careful walk. Time wasn't important out here. Indians preferred to wait things out. Time was more often to their advantage.

Our eyes met. And after some pause I offered a greeting in Cherokee, knowing they'd not understand, being this far west. Yet it was a way to avoid the use of English until communications deemed it necessary. Figured they'd see me not as one associated with the white man and his mounted soldiers.

"You ride white man's trail. Not one of us." The speaker sat on a large stallion, flanked on both side by his warriors. His hand gestured the country around us. "You come from east?"

I nodded. "That is so. Cherokee country. Very far." My words came slow and broken, hoping they might see me more as one of them.

"Why you ride like white man … over hard leather?" one of the warriors remarked. The others grinned mockingly at my saddle and stirrups.

"Part of the work I was hired to do. Herding cattle." I let the big one chew on that, then said: "A wagon train comes through peacefully. They offer gifts and shall leave your land … by nightfall tomorrow." I was thinking of our need to camp tonight. Figure we might avoid trouble when them wagons got this far into Ute country.

"You ride with them?"

"I do. For few days. I break off and travel north soon."

"What gifts they bring?" the leader asked.

I thought quickly about what I'd seen on board the wagons—items that might be useful to Indians of Mojave. "Meat. Blankets," I asserted.

"We shall wait."

I looked back over the trail. Wisps of dust rose up beyond a low ridge. "They come now."

When the wagons appeared, I rode back to collect what I could.

"The Utes demand gifts for passage," I told McCann. "They appear to be peaceful on those terms."

"That's bloody extortion!" Frank reined in and sat his bay.

"You'd have a hundred mile detour otherwise," I replied. "Better we cross their land."

Frank's face turned a bold red. "Over my dead—"

"Enough!" Tom McCann growled. "We'll pay it as a goodwill gesture." Tom twisted around and waved to the line of wagons. "Wrap some jerked beef, and round up four blankets. Keep everyone quiet, and have your rifles loaded and ready!"

Tom McCann cut from the group and rode down the line of the wagons to repeat his orders.

Soon women in the two lead-wagons were wrapping up several pounds of beef, and had folded four blankets. We loaded them on my roan. When I rode out to the war party they looked pleased. For it was better to eat well and sleep under a warm blanket at night, than to fight against many guns and risk a death among the clan. I could see the Utes were smart and they knew how to pick their battles.

We parted ways with signs of peace. I sat my roan off to the side, watching the Utes ride out of sight. The wagon train hit the dusty trail west.

Mojave Crossing

An hour later we found ourselves in a sea of endless sand, dotted by an occasional Joshua tree and much prickly pear. The sun was high and the livestock were slowin' down a mite. Thunderheads churned towards the mountains to our right. What was left of that range broke off to the desert floor westward. I kept my eyes open for shade and any evidence of desert springs. The animals would be needing to stop no less than twice a day if we kept this pace during daylight hours.

Billy appeared at my side on a paint he rode when his ma allowed him to venture out. "Mister Llano, how do Injuns stay alive in the desert?"

Now that was a loaded question for me to tackle. "The Cherokee never lived in the desert, but I reckon them tribes living out here know a sight about edible plants and where to find water."

Billy thought about that. "So then, how are we going to know what to eat if we run out of what we took out here?"

"That's a very smart question, and I'd hoped, betwixt the men and women folk, someone would know more'n the rest of us. However, I did learn a thing or two from books I read back in

Prescott. Yuh know, a fella can learn much if he's willing to read, Billy."

We rode in silence for several minutes, until I pointed out what I'd been looking for. "Yuh see that cactus over yonder? That's what they call Yucca. It's got some edible flowers and even fruit growin' on it."

"I don't cotton much to all them thorns," Billy replied.

"Nor do I, Billy. Fella's gotta handle 'em right careful when he plucks off the edible parts. I reckon we'll git us a few on the trip."

After a spell, Billy dropped back to the wagons. I rode on ahead to explore the ground beyond the dunes we was nearin'. Our plan was to cut north once we got shut of the mountains looming off to our right. Then we'd pick up the Bradshaw Trail and continue west toward Los Angeles.

Folks claimed it was well traveled and we'd have a better chance at watering our stock at a series of springs along the way. Tom had avoided a place called La Paz on account of some trouble with Mojaves, folks going east was talkin about. Me, I ain't seen hide nor hair of Indian folk since we left them Utes. Figured we'd be better off on the trail, but I kept my thoughts to myself when Tom and Fred made up their minds to wander south.

We was feelin' the effects of the mid-afternoon blazing sun, and the lack of hydration that come with it. So I let Smoke have his head as we come by a patch of yucca and mesquite, thinkin' he might smell water and take me there.

Sure as cactus have thorns he veered off toward them scrubby mesquite trees and dropped his head over a seep of water coming up through some rocks in the shade. Now it wasn't much, but enough to keep him going for a spell.

I waved the first wagon over and the rest followed right quick. We stopped and decided on camping right then and there. The men pulled shovels out and we commenced to digging us a trench. A'fore long water just come a bubblin' up right out of the ground! A good bit of water for the livestock, figgering we'd rotate them in shifts.

But some of the oxen got mighty rambunctious when they smelled that water, so we had to let 'em git to it or they was gonna tear the wheels off the wagons.

The next morning come early and we was moving almost due north to pick up that Bradshaw Trail. I believe it was a few of the strong-headed women folk who talked some sense into the men in charge cuz we lit out of there at a good pace and everybody was a cheering 'cept Tom McCann and Fred Murphy. They was scowlin' like a schoolmarm sittin' on a tack.

Didn't matter to me much how we got across that desert so I just taken up the lead and went to doing my job. One of the dogs in the group, he took to my roan and follered us yonder.

I watched him chase down a pack rat or two after they scattered from some shady cover where they was resting. Varmints move quick enough to leave that hound dog in the dust.

By lunch time we'd hooked up with the Bradshaw Trail and were again pointed west. The road was decent, and I guessed we was makin' better time than yonder over rough ground.

The drivers pulled the wagons off the trail and under a stand of cottonwoods. We let the livestock drink after the ladies filled the water jugs from a spring that come out the side of a small ridge. Them cottonwoods are a sure sign of water pert-near anywhere you go. And the way our horses' ears pricked up with nostrils distended, we knew there was a plenty.

The children lit out for the trees and were singing from the branches b'fore the women had bread and jerked beef laid out. Billy, he come over to me askin' about a big old cactus growin' yonder, maybe a hundred yards. That monster was all topped with heavenly flowers in a swell of devil's thorns.

"A barrel cactus," I told him. "Not much for water like you'd think being so big and fat." Nonetheless, he was mighty curious so he turned on his heel to run have a look.

I was rubbing down Smoke when I heard the cry. Billy was standing stark still and whimpering. I seen him pointing at the ground near that barrel cactus.

Well, I was no stranger to snakes, which was exactly what he'd stumbled upon. I reached for my Winchester and come within ten yards of him when I seen that big rattler a waggin' his tail, all coiled up and lookin' Billy square in the eye.

"Easy, boy," I told him in a low voice. "You just back up right slow and easy."

Billy did as I said, taking one step, then another … and that durned rattler, he raised his head like he was going to strike as sure as mud in a rainstorm. My gun was up and drawing a bead on that old boy. "Keep a goin' Billy. Git out of his range and he'll cool off."

Billy, he just kept a backin' up real slow like. Now I seen it … that snake's head start to drop back to the ground. As for Billy, he was shakin' like a leaf in a hurricane when he turned and run over to me.

"That was all mighty close," I sighed. "He had yuh dead to rights, and if you hadn't stopped where you did— Anyways, yuh done good, boy."

By the time we sat down to lunch Billy was feelin' a mite better and did he have a story to tell! His ma was pale as a sheet when she heard about that rattler. "It's okay, Ma. A body can't never ignore his instincts out here. That's what Mister Llano taught me."

"Well, I'm much obliged to him. He ain't always gonna be there to save your life. Nevertheless, I thank him for goin' out there like he did. I'm indebted."

"Ain't nothin', ma'am. Reckon it's my job to see folks is safe out here. And this jerked beef you served up, it's mighty tasty, ma'am."

She smiled and we all ate in silence, figgering we'd a few blessings to count.

Before sundown we pulled off the trail into a canyon and made camp. I estimated we'd come a good twenty miles since breakfast under some cloud cover. Wasn't bad for a day's worth of dusty travel. Them livestock were mighty glad to be shut of that trail.

I watered the mules and oxen, rubbed down my horse, and was fixin' to demolish them slabs of beef all smothered in beans they was servin' round the campfire. Billy, he come over and set up on a rock and commenced to devourin' his plate of eggs and beef like no tomorrow. The other men and I just chuckled as we watched him.

"Grub goes down that boy like a dose of sauce through a widow-woman," I remarked.

His ma smiled proudly. "And he'll be startin' all over again by sun-up."

Billy, he sat a-grinning at me, gravy running down his chin. "Yup."

That was all Billy said, b'fore following it down with a jar of fresh goat's milk. I turned to his ma. "That's a growin' boy yuh got there. Fine lad he'll turn out to be if he works as much as he eats!"

His ma nodded and ate quietly. That's when Billy asked me about my guns, figgerin' it was time to have a couple of his own.

"Boy, there ain't no purpose to carryin' around these here six-shooters, 'less you know how to treat 'em. Too easy to git yourself hurt ... or killed if you was to cross the wrong feller.

"You see, a man's gotta keep his cool while others are out building a reputation. Don't be settin' store by no foolish gun-play. It's a sure way to the grave ... or to the jailhouse if you pull that trigger on an innocent man."

"Why do you carry 'em?" he asked directly.

"You seen the way that rattler come up ready to strike. A gun is right handy out on the range. Reckon I been a mite lucky to never kilt nobody. Blowed off some fingers and busted a hand or two, but I ain't put nobody in the ground, and I intend to keep it that way."

Billy, he just nodded and was back to them beans rollin' around his plate. After I seen him takin' a fancy to my irons, I wanted him to know guns have their use, but there's a lot more to a real man than branding himself a fast-draw. Tends to attract some unwanted challenges from fellers lookin' to carve them out a name on the range.

I wasn't sure Billy could see all I was a preachin'. His ma sure enough did, cuz when I got up for another cup of coffee, why she was a smilin' like I'd been reading gospel straight from the Book.

Two days on the trail passed with no sign of Indian or foe. The wagons had covered but thirty miles at my best estimate. Days of blazing sun forced us to camp up against any ridge we could find that pushed up from the basin into the desert, and then travel by night.

Water was in short supply on the third day so I'd volunteered to scout on ahead, cutting off the trail to the north in search of a spot called Coyote Springs. It was an unusually dry year according to folks traveling east. Three tanks along the trail known for having water had turned up dry. That suddenly put us at risk of losing more livestock if we didn't find water soon.

Smoke had a good nose for water and so I gave him his head as we topped a rise and dipped down among scattered mesquite and prickly pear over a broken raw landscape. Trouble was, he didn't show interest in any particular direction.

I finally swung down next to a patch of ocotillo and with the tip of my bowie knife extracted enough water to wet my parched mouth. My eyes searched desperately for patches of green that might produce a hat full of water for the roan.

The desert air was heavy with hardly a breeze to offset the radiant heat of the late afternoon sun. A mile or two away from the wagons, a shallow wash lie yonder to my right. On foot I walked the roan to the sandy bank and dropped to my knees. My canteen sloshed but an ounce of water. Coyote Springs was said to be at a bend in the wash under a stand of cottonwoods, but I saw nothing of the sort.

Had I taken a wrong turn?

A hoof striking stone turned my head in time to see the glint of a rifle barrel swing up behind a lone boulder. Its report followed the burn across my skull, leaving me face down in the sand.

Making no movement, I listened, waited. Nothing could be heard for several minutes. But I sensed the presence of another man nearby. Finally the hoof falls of a horse retreated down the gravely wash.

Who had come and taken a shot at me, then left me for death in the scorching heat?

All my remaining strength went into thinking. For a man cannot survive without thinking through his adversities. First, I assessed my condition. Aside from a desperate need for water, I realized my bullet wound was largely superficial—a furrowed cut along the side of my head that left my hair matted with blood. I would survive, only if I found water. Soon!

I crawled on my belly to the sparse shade of a mesquite tree inhabited by scrawny manzanita growing in the bottom of a shallow depression in the wash. There I slept soundly. Consciousness returned to me suddenly, for the air had changed, with a cold dampness falling over me. Rain? The air smelled of it and no stars glimmered in the midnight sky, my ears keen to the utter silence that embraced me.

I detected no sounds one might expect from creatures of the night on the desert floor. For scorpions, snakes, and other nocturnal predators would surely be actively seeking their next meal. Then it came to me.

A storm was brewing!

As sudden as the thought came to me, the sky burst open with searing fingers of lightning smashing down upon the desert floor with rapid thunderous crashes. The open desert was illuminated for seconds at a time, showing miles of white sandy dunes to the west, and jagged peaks to the distant north.

A spattering of drops danced over me, rapidly turning to torrential sheets of rain. In the space of halted time, I lay blissfully rejoicing in the sands.

Shifting sands!

The wet sand had folded beneath me, and drifted in all directions. My body shivered violently as a powerful wind spat sand and debris into my face, blinding me. By now the heat of the lightning had chilled thoroughly with speed.

Suddenly I realized the real danger of lying in the bottom of a wash. This desert riverbed would be an overflowing deluge in minutes, sweeping me to my death if I failed to move to higher ground!

I struggled to my feet, stumbling over the barren rocks, exposed by the violent wind that accompanied the downpour. With a fight I reached the bank and crawled up to its rim, panting under vicious streaks of lightning tearing at trees and cactus within yards of where I rested.

A dozen yards further I reached the outline of a sandy ridge, at the base of which was littered with boulders, smoothed over by millennia of wind, rain, and harsh desert temperatures. There I managed to pull myself up to a high point just as the roar of a mad locomotive charged down the gully. The rush of churning water inches from my toes lashed at its banks. Angry groans of snapping tree branches and twisted cactus passed by as they were carried away in the distance.

The sudden crash of deafening fury lit up the sky, giving me a brief glimpse of a burning barrel cactus tumbling off a ridge. In that moment I was suddenly struck by debris and buried under soggy earth. Darkness and silence enveloped me.

Cactus Valley

"That you, Mister Llano?" The voice bellowed over me, familiar and right welcoming.

I don't know how long I was out but it was daylight and the sun was beating down on my curled up frame, covered with mud and silt from the wash that had now shrunk to little more than a creek.

Billy Nevil swung down off the bay and slipped over the bank to where I lay, lookin' feeble and helpless. "Thought you was cut down by Injuns after taking out on your own a couple days back. Folks in the train figured you'd done left us, Mister Llano."

I stumbled to my feet and braced myself against a twisted greasewood, wiping off the sand and mud. "Someone took a shot at me. Burned me across the scalp. Lost my horse."

Billy smiled. "We found him. He come back our way 'bout the time our wagon busted a wheel."

I took up my hat and beat it on a rock. "Reckon everybody's yonder, waitin' on me."

He looked at me kinda serious. "Nope." Billy was shaking his head. "Train done went on without us."

"What?"

"Yup. Folks got sceer'd of being washed out or trapped during the rain, and hightailed it."

Your ma okay?"

Billy nodded. "She's a fixin' grub over yonder. Reckon she'll be relieved, on account of us needing some help with that busted wheel."

Billy rode back while I washed up in the creek, for the water ran clear now. The scar on my head had already scabbed over. The creek water tasted cool and sweet.

When I walked into their camp Billy's ma come out from behind the wagon fussin' over me. "We thought you was lost or shot up."

I nodded to her. "Reckon you is right, on account I *was* lost for a spell, and someone did take a shot at me." Sitting on a boulder near the fire I drank from the cup Billy's mother handed me. "Yuh see, a feller can git hisself in some trouble out here, just like I did. Better to stay close, like your ma says, Billy."

"We got your horse, Llano. He come right back where we was camped during that storm. I got him ground hitched round back of the wagon."

"I appreciate that, young feller. E'vry man needs a friend like you around."

We broke camp after repairing the broken wheel and found our way back to the main trail. Wispy clouds hung lazily as we plodded westward. I rode back a ways so I could take in the country and watch our back trail. The scab under my hat kept me thinkin' about that unknown gunman. Just the three of us were alone out here now, and if someone was lookin' to make trouble I'd have to be ready for it.

Late afternoon I was riding back a ways when we come up over a high ridge. Billy was sitting with his legs dangling over the back of the wagon, looking through his glass scope across the brush flats below. His ma was at the reins.

Before I knew it, one of their mules suddenly rears up and jerks the wagon off the trail and down the steep hillside, leading the team with it. So I put spurs to my horse and raced to catch up, only to see the wagon take a final bounce and slam into an outcrop of boulders. In good fortune, Billy had tumbled off the back of the wagon before it had gone far.

He was on his feet in a dead run behind me, down the slope to the bottom of the ravine. Fearing the worst, I caught up Billy when I seen his ma lying twisted amongst the boulders. There was nothing we could do. Her final plea was to rear the boy up right.

His screaming eventually melted into sobs, and by sundown he struggled to occupy himself with the chores of gathering wood for a fire and setting up camp. I dug the grave and we honed out a crucifix and come up with a prayer to recite over Mrs. Nevil.

Later that evening I did what could be done to repair the wagon's fractured axle. We took out north under the stars toward the mountains poking up across the far plains. The desert was behind us and our direction angled slightly east instead of toward the coast.

I'd seen nobody in that wagon train who cared enough to take in Billy. Most were tending to their young or lookin' to strike it big in gold country. Spots in California had played out, but occasional word got around of a silver strike or a gold vein that spurred folks to a frenzied migration.

Me, I didn't set store to mining. It was a life for some I'd met back in Arizona country. Maybe it was ranchin' I'd someday settled down to. First I had dreams of sailin' on the great sea. Suddenly that notion was growing dimmer.

Billy handled the reins behind four good oxen. The wagon carried an ample supply of grub and what other possessions that hadn't been smashed against the rocks.

"Keep a good eye out for rattlers," I told him. "I suspect that's what frightened the animals while going over that ridge. Them snakes sun themselves on high points, and I should've thought of that."

I rode within view of Billy, watching for water and places to camp while he kept the wagon aimed at the mountains. Three days passed with no sign of human life in any direction.

We come up over a ridge and paused near a stand of pines when I seen four riders running their horses hard across a wide valley below us.

Dust stirred up as they cut into a trail that ran straight for about two miles until it bent eastward into a small town.

Taking our time, we followed that trail and crossed a creek meandering out of a hollow along side a canyon peppered with cactus and mesquite. Cloud shadows blotted out the barren ground as we plodded on. A cool breeze blew from the west.

Then we seen their sign: *Cactus Valley*.

We walked alongside our stock as we come into town. On the main street folks were about. We stopped at a water trough across from the bank and a clapboard hotel. Tents and a few shanty buildings lined one side of the street toward the end of town.

A livery with a pole-corral out back bordered the creek. Next to it was a blacksmith and a general store, both buildings bleached out by the blazing sun. An eating house had been erected across the way. A stream of dusty miners and motley drifters flowed in and out of a saloon. It was called the Hitching Post, the largest of three gambling establishments in a stretch of two blocks.

By the time our oxen had their fill, we'd seen a good part of the town come and go—some the likes of upstanding citizens with a purpose to grow the little startup town. Others had a notion to take what they could and leave.

Billy and me, we stood there and watched one roistering lot ride in from the hills west.

Cactus Valley had some side streets that ran into the main drag, and there were at least two alleys that ran out toward the creek and some pastures on both sides of town.

From another direction, three galoots come up the street whooping it up, firing pistols into the air. Their mounts kicked up clouds of blowing dust as they drew up in front of the Hitching Post.

The townspeople walking along the boardwalks scattered and ducked into doorways as the three gents popped off more shots, then looked around to fancy their handy work. A tall lanky man wearing a black vest caught my eye. His strong jawbones chewed and spat beneath brutal white eyes. Turning toward the street, he tossed his head in laughter, then pushed through the batwing doors into the Hitching Post. His partners, two powerful hombres, dirty and unshaven, followed him inside, one pausing to slap the buttocks of a lady trying to get out of the way.

This obnoxious demeanor rankled me, and got me wondering about the jailhouse, which looked to be abandoned.

And no sign of a lawman.

Sure, there was a time to blow off steam and make a ruckus, but not when it jeopardized the rights of decent people building a future for the town.

No sign of the law meant what?

Few amongst the town folk looked able or willing to stand up to the bullies and trouble hunters we'd seen in the minutes we'd stood at the trough. The noise inside the saloons was constant, explosive. Yet it was barely past noon! I could only imagine these same characters carryin' on after nightfall.

I had Billy turn the wagon into some shaded ground along the creek bed. He ground-hitched the livestock. We were good and hungry and hadn't a real meal in several days, not since the day Billy's ma got throwed off the wagon.

We dusted ourselves off. Billy beat the Stetson hat his pa had given him on his denim jeans. He stuck it back on his head, pullin' it back a mite and smiled up at me feeling right proud.

That boy was a survivor.

I hitched up my guns and bunched my hair up under my hat, then we walked into the eatin' house. The sign out front read:

Darla's Diner,
25 cents a plate.
No Liquor Served!

The lady who ran the place wanted no trouble and made it clear enough for folks to abide. Inside, a young girl about Billy's age come over to greet us. She wiped her hands on her apron, then looked Billy up and down with big eyes. Gathering her wits, she recited the menu.

"Reckon I'll git me a plate of beef 'n beans. As for you, Billy, what'll it be?"

"Sand-wich," was all that come out of his mouth. His eyes was wide and gazin' all about the place … like he ain't never been in a restaurant in all his days. Finally, I grinned up at the young girl. "Beef sandwich for my partner, ma'am. Extra sauce."

Billy smiled at that and watched the girl skip off to the kitchen.

"I believe she has an eye for you, boy."

He flushed red in the cheeks but said nothin'. Just sat there watching folks hurry along the street and past the windows. Inside the place was cool and clean with few patrons.

Two ladies occupied themselves with gossip in a corner of the room while a couple of businessmen smoked cigars over mumbled talk of how too many outsiders were takin' over the town.

Reckon it was that way everywhere there was talk of gold. Still, folks don't cotton much to changes, especially when it means more strangers pouring in. I listened with interest, but it was hard to hear much over the ruckus outside. Drunken miners occasionally firing off their pistols and whooping it up in the street.

Was this how these little California towns conducted their business?

There was a fight heating up in the street 'bout the time a buxom middle-aged woman brought us our food. That was my chance to make inquiries.

"You must be Darla. Pardon me for sayin' so', but we ain't seen hide nor hair of the law since we come to town. What with all the roistering and shootin', you folks must have a sheriff or a marshal here in Cactus Valley."

Pursing her lips, Darla shook her head: "Last two marshals on that job are lying side by side in Boot Hill, and one before them was run clean out of town."

"That's mighty unfortunate, ma'am. How's a town to git along like this?"

"Power and money," she answered flatly. "It's that Henry Drake teaming up with a proprietor named Vance Stromberg. They're poison mean but they got a lot of money, so they more or less run the town. Some say they jumped the best gold claims and ran the good men out … or had them killed."

"Any decent fellers with some pull around here?" I asked casually.

"A few tough landowners are all we got to keep the lid from blowin' off … but they're too busy feuding over water rights."

"A cross b'twixt bad and worse."

Darla smiled non-committedly and drifted over to the table where the ladies had been sitting.

Billy and me, we dug into our grub in silence. Gave me a chance to do me some thinkin' about what I was gonna do with the boy before I'd…

"Dos tequila, por fa'vor! ... Means two sippin' whiskeys, in *greaser* talk." The first one roared to his partner as the two hombres come crashing through the front door.

"Them Mexicans sure do talk funny."

"I want *my* whiskey on rye!" the first one laughed

Both had a snoot full. And by the way them two staggered in and plopped down at a table near the window, I was bracin' for trouble.

Suddenly, Darla come bustin' out of the kitchen waving a quirt. "We don't serve liquor here ... and I don't allow drunks in my diner. Get out!"

My palm slid down over my pistol and released the thong that held it down—a habit that come to me years back when trouble was about. Billy, he just stared at that woman, unbelieving. Reckon he'd never seen the likes of her ... or this crazy town.

I sat there grinning at her spunk as my heart raced and hackles sprouted up my back. A hyped readiness stirred inside me. For I had a stern distaste for a man's rudeness and disrespect, especially toward a lady proprietor.

The big-mouth blond rose to his feet and glared over at me and Billy.

"What are *you* lookin' at?"

Seeing my face unreadable, he turned back to Ms. Darla. "Ain't goin' no-where, ma'am ...

not til I git me a drink and mebbe a dance with the pritty lady!"

Seeing nothing of the cowering response he expected from a woman, big blond's menacing blue eyes grew cold and ugly. The handlebar mustache under his crooked nose twitched nervously. Swaying side to side, he waited for her to back down.

That Ms. Darla had sand!

She took two bold steps toward him and pointed at the door with the quirt. "This is no drinking establishment. And I don't dance with dogs. So beat it."

"… and if we don't?" He turned grinning back at his pal.

"Then *I'll* throw you out on yer ass!"

The growl bellowed across the room in a tone I'd not heard of a man of my years. Now big blond, he spun around to face me, all wicked eyed. I was on my feet a body's length behind Darla, angled to her left.

"Now dere's some thing I wanna see!" he grunted slowly. "A whoopin' from a *breed*."

But his eyes lost some of their ambition as he surveyed my narrow hips and broad shoulders, for I was built well beyond the average lean Indian, but my face said otherwise; bronze with prominent cheekbones. Coal black hair spilling from under my black-crowned hat. A breed I was … with enough Irish fight in me to beat him clean across the Pecos.

I glimpsed his partner to see if there'd be any gunplay in this little scuffle, but neither of 'em wore guns. Big blond's pal had sobered up a mite, shuffling toward the front door.

I wasn't lookin' to maim or kill, just willing to rough up any man who took the liberties to ignore this lady's house rules.

Darla could sense the danger in the belligerent man drooling over her. And she sensed I needed more space to intervene, so she scooted back out of my way.

With lightning speed and a clear path, I stepped in toward big blond and delivered a powerful right to his jaw, shaking him to his knees. But he rose quickly in a trembling chorus of muscles and madness, and let loose a wild round house right that whistled in the air over me. A clean miss as I ducked, then I landed a wicked blow to his wind. He doubled over slightly before taking up a wooden chair in his massive hands.

The chair exploded over the floor as I side stepped it, and I returned with a well-planted left, followed by a series of right-handed sucker punches. He went down in a heap and before he had time to recoil, I grabbed him by the scuff of the collar and dragged him out the door.

When his buddy come through, my eyes met him with authority.

He shook a finger at me. "We'll be back, Injun boy. Back for you later!"

"Now's as good as any, ain't it?"

He said nothing to my challenge, but I could see the devil's contempt in his eyes. He was a tactful man who could wait. A man who yearned for brawlin' when the cards were stacked in his favor … with a gun on his hip.

Billy was standing inside the door when I come back inside. Darla stood behind him, her hands on his shoulders in a protective gesture.

"You need not have done that, Mister …?"

"Name's *Llano*, ma'am."

Billy, he piped up right quick: "They call him the *Llano Kid*, ma'am. He's the one people say can shoot the gun out—."

"That's enough, Billy," I coughed. "No point in bustin' open the whole watermelon."

Darla smiled but it wasn't a happy smile. "That's nice, Billy," she with a glare in my direction. "This town is no place for a bold man to take a stand. There are too many bad ones who will just cut him down like a dog. I suggest you both ride out of here before they come back with more of the same lot."

"I do appreciate your concern, ma'am, but we ain't leavin' so soon. In fact, we like it here."

I didn't know exactly what made me say that to her cuz I did not like what I saw in Cactus Valley. Maybe it was all about filling a need.

Billy and me, we finished our meal without a word but my thoughts were on what the lady had said. It rankled because I wasn't one to run away from trouble when it called and needed to be confronted.

We got up and I paid for our food. Darla thanked me and smiled at Billy. From inside looking out, I felt something bad brewing on the street. So I told Billy to slip out the backdoor and return to the wagon. I'd be along later.

When the backdoor slammed behind him I hitched up my guns and checked my loads. From inside the front window, out of the line of fire, my eyes searched the street. The scene outside appeared worse now, with an outlaw element gathering. There was no longer any sign of law-abiding folk. No doubt, a showdown was building.

Was it something amongst themselves? Or was it me they wanted? I hadn't been in town long enough to learn their patterns, but I was willing to bet on the latter. I'd seen Indians and Mexicans beat up or gunned down by mobs of such, more than once.

The deuces I'd run out of Darla's were licking their wounds and ranting on about that durn Injun in the diner. At least a dozen miners loafed in the street. Others loitered further down in front of the gamblin' joints—tough unkempt men with battered clothes, and well-worn six-shooters on their hips. Men eager to blow off steam.

Would there be an ambush the moment I stepped out onto the boardwalk in front of Darla's place? In this town, what was one more dead man?

How many had died here at the hands of greed and bad whiskey already?

But my number wasn't up.

Nor was a pointless battle to take place at Darla's Diner. And I whispered as much to her.

"I want you to close up for the afternoon." Then I spoke briefly of my plan."

She hesitated, then pulled her apron strings loose and handed me a key to the front door. Upon locking it I escorted her and the young girl working there out the backdoor. We hurried along the backstreet to a small house she indicated was her grandfather's place.

"Go inside and don't come out until this mob is dispersed," I told her.

Then, circling around the outskirts of town, I found myself behind the jailhouse. A side door was busted in, so I could enter quietly. The jail cells were littered with trash and the place smelled musty.

With not a sound I surveyed the contents of the office. The ammunition and rifles had been looted from locked storage cabinets. Rats had chewed through the leather desktop. A steel marshal's badge lay on the wooden floorboards.

The building had seen little use for weeks, if not longer. In a drawer I found keys, which I tried on the cell doors. They worked. Without wasting a minute, I swept out the cells and got to work organizing the office. Surprisingly the front door was locked and the wooden structure was solid.

The men loitering outside Darla's stood with their backs to the jailhouse, expecting me to come out of the restaurant. But they were liquored up and had lost track of time, thinking I'd eventually play right into their hands.

Finally, someone called me out of Darla's. Another cussed and made threats. Soon, others joined in as I watched carefully from the dusty desk inside the marshal's office. I studied their movements, seeking the man with authority in the group. When it came time to lay down the law, he would be my prime target.

Was I crazy … or just a gentleman fool?

Justice was born and bred into me … and now I had thoughts of ... Could I ever get away with it? Would the town mayor approve of what I was about to do? Was there a mayor in Cactus Valley? Darla had never mentioned one.

My head swam with what-ifs as I watched the drunken miners pop off more shots and cuss loudly, biding their time with open threats directed at the *Injun* using the diner as a hideout.

Deep inside my gut something gradually drove me to action. Was it the many law-abiding towns folk trying to go about their business in Cactus Valley—women like Darla who ran respectable businesses?

Had this been a rough-shod mining camp of only lawless miners, I'd give no more thought but to ride on, taking Billy with me. Such start-ups were common; many died off, while others blossomed into thriving townships.

There was Billy. Leaving him to grow up here would be a moral dilemma. He needed a good home to bring him along. Since the death of his kin, it was on my shoulders to see to it the boy got a fair shake; some social guidance from a mother figure. Soon enough I'd say goodbye to Billy and leave him to grow up like a boy should.

From the fussin' and carrying on I'd been watching in the street, I soon had me a hunch of who their ring leader was. The one in that lot who'd come riding into town when we was waterin' our stock at the trough.

Watchin' this man parade around like the cock-of-the-walk nagged at me. Suddenly I knelt down and took up that badge lying there on the floor. From a shadow inside the window I mentally cataloged the men, their manner, and their hardware.

When I stepped out of the marshal's office with that badge hangin' on my buckskin vest and my guns hung low, they hardly knowed what hit 'em. And so that's how it happened that I became acting marshal of Cactus Valley.

I stood, unseen on the boardwalk fronting the office, when a pack of them boys goes troopin' up and starts banging on the diner's front door. "Send the Injun out, Miss Darla," the tall one shouted. "We ain't after nobody but that breed. Got my own way of handlin' trouble in this town."

I stepped down onto the street and took three steps toward the crowd.

"And I got *my* own way of ending it!"

The crowd looked side to side, confused of where the words had come from. My Texas spurs jingled to the rhythm of my footsteps. Now I stood twenty yards from the line of gunmen. Facing me, utterly shocked at what they saw, their ranks spread out over the street's broad width.

The badge on my breast pocket glinted in the afternoon sun. It represented a new command in Cactus Valley.

The self-appointed leader of this ugly lot in the black vest had situated himself in the middle. His hands spread out, indicating he was in charge, and I was for his taking.

"Who the hell are *you*?" He sneered. "Don't recall givin' no Injun the privilege of wearin' a marshal's badge in Cactus."

"They call me the Kid, the Llano Kid."

Suddenly he paled, then quickly composed himself. Glaring at one of his partners, he growled: "Thought you left him in the desert for—".

"—for dead?" my tone was cold, dry.

I eagle-eyed him, remembering the rifle shot I'd taken down by the wash. I'd been stalked and assumed dead by one in this wicked lot.

"Life is full of surprises, ain't it?

Their leader wore an ugly sneer upon his face, and I wasn't sure if his contempt was greater for me or for his partner who'd bragged about killing the Llano Kid back at camp.

"Why don't you *try* it marshal?"

The others moved well off to the side. That's when I noticed a couple of men in broadcloth suits standing alongside the buildings, rifle in hand. My guess was they were *not* with these rawhide hombres, but rather the landowners Darla had spoken of.

I gambled on the notion they'd back me up, or at least serve as a deterrent to dirty play.

"We'll do it my way." My reply came out matter-of-fact. "I'm gonna count. You either ride … or start shooting b'fore I git to *ten*."

The tall one, he didn't expect this. Not from a stranger half-breed in town, wearing a marshal's badge. It rankled him and the fury in his eyes showed it.

I began counting, knowing this could be my final breath.

No matter. I had a job to do … and I'd opened the ball. "Three … four … " I counted slow and easy, ready as I could be for him to draw.

But he stood there looking me over, unsure of where I'd been … and who I was. When I got to *seven*, his hand swept down for iron.

My right gun came up, my left hand working the hammer as I leveled the barrel on his hands. His gun spouted flame, and a slug whizzed by my ear, another tugged at my shirt sleeve. Suddenly he was standing in disbelief, both his pistols lying on the dusty street in front of his feet. One hand was bathed in blood.

"Marshal done shot the guns right out of my hands!" he shouted.

I walked forward and holstered my gun, my eyes wary of the others flanking me on both sides. They all seemed astonished that a man could stop another man like I had done … with no killing!

I picked up his two guns and glanced at each of the others. Holster them guns, boys. And from now on you'll leave 'em quiet unless you have to defend yourself. If you can't foller them rules I take 'em away. Got it?"

Without a word, the men dispersed. Some I didn't see for days. The two suited men with rifles approached me later, introducing themselves, a rancher and the owner of the general store. I stated my intent to stick around until a permanent lawman could be hired. My wages would come from ordinary taxes. I'd keep a room inside the jailhouse.

Later that afternoon I circulated about the town, greeted by citizens who thanked me for my bold efforts. Word got around mighty quick about my square shootin' which seemed to quiet the lawless ones … for the time being.

Later I saw the big blonde man—the one I'd sucker punched over at Darla's place. He eyed me real evil like, and I reminded him of who's in charge here. B'twix the grunts and the evil looks, I knew I wasn't shut of him.

Darla took in Billy, and he was soon learning to read along with Lizzy, the girl who helped Darla at the diner. Billy seemed happy with his new friends, but I knew he needed some confidence before I could pull up stakes and leave.

The boy was eager to learn at the little schoolhouse and he caught on fast. He started deciphering books right away. Lizzy had learned a mite and the two were happy to read to each other at night in front of Darla and when they called on her grandfather for a visit.

Billy and I agreed to pay Darla the money we got for selling the wagon and the oxen. Some of that money would be set aside for Billy when he struck out on his own someday.

He and I often rode out on the prairie where I taught him more about the gun—how to respect it and use it proper like. We also talked about hunting small game and deer. I taught him how to stalk the animal, unseen. "When he's eating that's when you move in. Watch his tail. It starts a swishin' means he suspects danger. Then his head comes up. That's when you stand still. Wait till he goes back to grazin' before you move in closer."

We shot us one and dressed it out there on the hillside. Billy, he was mighty proud to be the one pulling the trigger on that buck. On the way back to town I pointed out some edible plants that have saved many a feller's life on the range.

"Over yonder, that *Indian thistle* is a staple. The roots are edible, as most flowers of cactus are south of here," I told him.

Cactus Valley was chiefly a mining town, in its humble beginnings. But many of the grounded folks living there now had come as outfitters, selling tools, grub, clothes, and all kinds of products that miners needed as they flooded into town. Those proprietors were as much the driving force to township maturity as the miners and prospectors had been.

In 1876 Cactus Valley had not only a small schoolhouse, but a church and a bank. A few ranches sprung up outside of town, supplying beef and bringing investment money to the town as its population grew to over two hundred year-round residents. The miners came and went, some moving on north and east into Nevada where news of pay-dirt was still making it around the campfires.

My job as marshal settled in after a few weeks of weeding out the hard-bitten hombres determined to run things their own way. Gambling attracted some of the bad element in the three saloons that hosted games and sold whiskey on the cheap. I'd seen some dirty dealing at the tables that too often erupted into gunplay and murder in cold blood.

The town's people were now paying me a hundred dollars a month to finish what I'd started that day I stood up against the gunman known as Judd Reese. No doubt he'd return for me ... once his hand healed over from my bullet. Killing another man without hesitation or remorse was in men like Reese.

Couple of his riders were getting' a mite restless one evening, determined to challenge my "no shooting" rule in town. The saloons were in full swing, and I was doing my rounds when I heard the shots.

Three trigger-happy hombres were puttin' holes in the boardwalk outside Darla's restaurant when I come up behind 'em.

"Hand them irons over, boys. You're played out tonight." My pistol was drawn, on account of their guns were out and shootin' up town property. "Drop your gunbelts, fellas. You can claim 'em back in the morning at the jailhouse."

One of 'em figured he could buck me for a fool, and said as much. "I don't take orders from no breed!"

"Mebbe not," I told him casually. "But you will take orders from the *law*."

I inched up closer, seeing he wasn't ready to back down. One of his pals had complied with my order and stepped back after his rig hit the dirt.

A third with keen eyes studied the odds, stepping behind the first one. He knew I had 'em dead to rights but wanted to see my sand.

In one swift motion my pistol swung up against the red-faced jowls of the big mouth man still clinging to his gun, which suddenly clattered onto the busted planks and through the hole he'd blasted open. Dropping to his knees, he cussed me out but made no trouble as I picked up the gun belts and their pistols.

"How 'bout *you*?" My eyes drilled the hold-out, now standing in the street. He was the brute who'd promised to come after me again the day I dragged his partner out of Darla's place.

Suddenly his gun fell to the dirt. "I'm done in for the night," he wheezed. "Reckon we'll be back in the morning to claim our stuff."

I gestured toward the shot-up boards. "Not till you gents repair the damage. Now, the lot of you, git."

I walked back to the office grinning to myself. Inside I hung their hardware on the remaining pegs screwed into the wall. There were others I'd taken that night—half dozen or more pistols, taken from insolent boys in big bodies.

The next day I paid a visit to the Rusty's Carpentry Shop. Rusty was an old fella who'd built near half the town. Nowadays he stuck to cabinets and tables.

"Hey, Llano, how's the marshallin' business today? Jailhouse full?" He was a cheerful old fellow, graying on the sides and bald on top. He was a man with a practical touch for doing things right.

"Got enough guns in there to fill a Texas armory," I replied wryly. "Need a favor."

"For you, anything! Can't thank you enough for takin' the bull by the horns. You be careful, Marshal. Plenty of trouble swirling around this here town."

"Can yuh make up three dozen wooden pegs, to start? The kind that screw into the wall."

He cocked his head. "Why, sure! Whatcha got in mind with all them pegs?"

"Got me a new law for this here town, Rusty. You make them pegs and I'll have the saloon owner drop by and pick 'em up. Have a bill ready for Vance Stromberg."

"You sure about that? I mean … Mister Stromberg, he don't—"

"Pay it no mind. You leave him to me."

Rusty was grinnin' ear to ear. "I git the picture, Marshal. I'll have 'em ready by dark."

"If our gamblin' joints start policing their patrons, I won't have to spend all my time rounding up firearms. Might save a few lives in the process."

Later that night I did my rounds to see that Rusty's hooks were put to use. The Hitchin' Post was my first stop. Inside it was smoky and noisy as ever. The tables were doing business at full tilt.

I glanced over at the bartender. He come over wiping his hands off on a towel.

"Evening, Marshal."

"Evening, Mel."

"At first, the boys didn't take to your new law, Marshal, but when I offered a free drink to anyone who'd use them hooks, why they unbuckled 'em up right quick."

"Good. A drinkin' man don't always use his best judgment," I replied quietly. "Better to keep them guns out of easy reach."

I glanced over a couple of poker games and walked out. The other saloons had followed suit and the town suddenly felt a bit more civilized. For how long, I'd no idea. Gambling and mining are a tough combination. Hard work, fast money, and sudden losses can bring out the poison in a man.

How long could I keep a lid on Cactus Valley? The town had good people but they were sandwiched between remnants of yesterday's rawhide outlaws. This place would either settle into a refined desert town, or go to hell in a handbasket. Depending on who possessed power and authority. For now it was up to me and a few others to keep a thumb on things. My mind was constantly anticipating what sort of trouble was coming next. For any marshal, keeping the peace was no easy task. For a breed out west? Life was a day-to-day question. Plenty of my foes grew up with Indians, good and bad.

One's attitude was based on personal experiences, and sometimes a little influence from other men who often didn't have the straight on things. Over all, a man's experience was his guide.

Several days passed with but a few encounters that needed some persuasion; little episodes of misguided ways and foolish thinking. And I found myself establishing new codes of conduct in light of safety, especially for the young'uns that were about. I reminded several shop owners to pick up their broken glass and other debris instead of sweeping it into the street. Simple stuff that some folks never thought through.

Other encounters involved outright challenges to the laws of reason and humanity.

One hot afternoon I come up on Stanley Webb, takin' a whip to his horse, cussing and carrying on.

"Now, what if that whip was to be turned on you?" I asked evenly. "Ain't never saw no sense in beating a horse lame, let alone any livestock."

The old man's back was to me as he spoke: "A man's got a right to discipline his animal, any which way he wants!" He paused, then suddenly that whip come around at my face.

"I don't need no two-bit—"

Half expecting this, my hand shot out, gathering in the leather fingers at the end of that horsewhip. With a firm yank I brought the old geezer to his knees.

"—two bit marshal enforcing the law, Mister Webb?" I growled. "This here town has some laws we all gotta live by. One of them laws is fair treatment of domestic animals. If I catch you at it again we'll hold us a public auction—sell off *all* your livestock."

"Getting to his feet, Webb protested. "You … you can't do that! Ain't no such law in Cactus Valley!"

"Is now. I wrote it into the town book of statutes this morning … after hearing 'bout the way you're abusing your stock."

He turned toward the neighbor's house, a small stone cabin with a flower garden out front and sneered. "Why … I'll git that little weasel of a—"

"Any more trouble out of you and I'll throw you in jail, after I tan your hide!"

I walked over to where the horse was standing in the corral, approaching him with a soft tone. He settled a bit, and my fingers probed his cinch. "Fine horse you got here, Stan. I reckon if you'd take that cinch out a mite, you'll get more cooperation out of him."

Webb, he pulled off his hat and slapped the dust out of it, shaking his head. I chuckled at the surprised look on his face. He then stomped off toward the house, grumbling under his breath.

"I'll be seeing yuh round, Stanley."

Every town had a horse-beater, most often the result of poor education on handling livestock proper like. I'd be paying old man Webb a visit occasionally.

Wheeling and Dealing

By sundown Cactus Valley was over-flowing with men. It wasn't just on the weekend. The mines were paying well, and so every night but Sunday was a gambling and drinking night in Cactus Valley. Friday was payday for most fellas, young and restless, with money to spend.

It was Friday evening when I come up the street for a meal. The music box was churning away in one joint, and a ranky-tanky piano in another. Loud voices of drunk or angry men spilled out through the open windows into the street.

I stepped up on the boardwalk and paused outside the Hitchin' Post looking to hear what the commotion was all about. First I hear Stromberg crooning over his gambling wheel.

"Around she goes … and where she stops, nobody knows!"

"Aah, put a sock in it!" someone hollered "The house *never* loses. Not on pay-day!"

"Ya!" growled a voice in the crowd. "Ain't never made me a dime on that durn wheel! Never seen that marble land on no miner's bets."

"You callin' me a liar and a crook?" Vance Stromberg's deep tone was firm, yet I picked up a hint of nerves. He was tall, handsome. The enterprising type, working the roulette wheel—a new gadget that some of the frontier gambling houses were making popular for those who didn't cotton much to cards and poker.

"I'm just callin' a spade a spade!"

"You can see as well as I can," Stromberg protested, "the *wheel* decides the winnings … as it does in any respectable gambling establishment."

"You'd think so." A powerful red-faced miner hunched over the table, glared at his money as it was scooped up and deposited into a steel strong box. "Somehow, I think you be cheatin us!"

Others chimed in and the place was in an uproar. After figgering on this problem, I walked in and stood by the door, taking it all in carefully. I had me a job to do b'fore the lid blowed clean off this little desert town.

Ever since I'd put myself in charge as marshal I had heard accounts of the miners losing their wages a lot more often than other gamblers who'd show up to patronize Stromberg's saloons once or twice a week.

While Vance Stromberg owned all three gamblin' joints, he rarely left the Hitching Post. This was odd to me … until I learned that he never put another man on the one roulette wheel he owned. I wondered about that, since it was a simple device to operate. Or was it?

Word had it Henry Drake who ran the only hotel in town had his fingers in the Stromberg's pie, somehow. He was said to back Stromberg whenever trouble come along … sometimes with a gun. Though I'd seen little of Drake lately.

Vance Stromberg was a powerful man with a shock of black wavy hair that hung over his cold eyes, one of 'em half closed. His beard was trimmed and combed neat against a pressed black shirt with green garters around the sleeves. He wore a Walker Colt in his waistband when the place was busy, and probably kept a loaded Derringer in his vest pocket … just in case.

I worked my way through the crowd. Men were huddled around Stromberg's gilded roulette wheel, sunk into a large table covered in green felt cloth, with numbers on a grid in red or black. Other betting options included any numbers *red, black, odd,* or *even.* While I had my hunches about Stromberg's operations, I wanted the dispute voiced peacefully, and for all to hear.

"What seems to be all the excitement here, gentlemen?" A few recognized me as the town's marshal while others scoffed at the notion.

One blowhard piped up ornery like: "What's it to you, half-breed?"

"Cuz I'm the marshal round here. You got an argument?" My eyes fixed coldly on him as he swallowed hard and backed off, his eyes sweeping from the badge on my buckskin vest down to my tied six-guns.

He suddenly grinned past two missing teeth. "Go ahead, Marshal, I ain't a stopping yuh."

The others turned their eyes back to Stromberg. "He's cheatin' us out of our pay, Marshal, and we aim to get it back!"

The others nodded. But Stromberg was in no mood for it. "Look here, Mister Llano. I run a respectable operation. I can't coddle a bunch of crybabies who come in here and lose their money. This is a *gambling* house!"

"A rigged one!" someone in the crowd shouted.

Stromberg flushed with fury. "Escort these gents out, Marshal! I can't have trouble every time some half-cocked miner loses a few bucks at the table."

The men grumbled amongst themselves. None was gonna be escorted out so easy. Not until they saw resolution or … some fair play.

I gestured for silence. "Alright, boys! Mister Stromberg says he runs an honest operation. Let's give him a chance to prove it."

Stromberg puffed on his black cigar and smiled. Had I detected contempt in his one sleepy eye … or was it just me?

I laid a dollar on the *odd number* tab, which would pay me back two bits over my dollar on any odd number. It was a small bet. A test bet. Stromberg spun the wheel, then let go a steel marble down a little ramp that angled toward a banked rim, fashioned around the outside of the dish-shaped roulette wheel. Carefully my eyes tracked the marble rolling in the opposite direction of the turning wheel. Could it somehow be controlled by some sleight-of-hand stunt Stromberg had up his sleeve? It all looked too random to be rigged.

Finally the marble dropped down into one of the slots matching the betting squares on the table. The number was *seven*. Stromberg picked up a little rake and shoved a two-bit coin and my dollar over to me.

"Marshal, you're a winner. Wanna let 'er ride?"

Shaking my head, I turned to the men gathered around the table. "Alright, who's next?"

A stout fella with a dark beard put down a shiny new gold piece. "Five dollars on black," he replied. His tone was skeptical. "That's all I got, Marshal."

My head cocked to one side, and I looked him in the eye. "Mister, you got almost half a chance to win ... and another half to *lose*, the way I see it."

"I just seen *you* win," he replied. "So I figger the wheel is workin' right fair for me!"

I said nothing more, knowing gamblin' is what they say it is. A man's luck can turn on him faster than a toilet-stop in rattlesnake country. I kept my eyes on Stromberg's fingers, searching for any movement that might suggest foul play.

Friend of mine back in Arizona played piano down in New Orleans. And he told me stories of gamblin' wheels down there controlled to favor the house. Something to do with magnetic slots and trick marbles.

But I knew little about that sort of thing, so I had no case against Stromberg. At least not at the moment. Besides, Stromberg was too smart to try anything foolish today, not with all them eyes on him and his wheel.

Stromberg spun the wheel again. The steel marble ran its course and dropped into a black number. "Another winner!" Stromberg crowed and paid up.

I thanked Vance and walked out.

No more trouble was heard from the Hitching Post that day, but I had me a sight of work to do. My own suspicions were that Stromberg was manipulating his games, one way or other.

I'd no sooner stepped out of the Hitching Post and walked along toward the jailhouse when an old-timer come up alongside me in the dark. He was speaking from the side of his mouth, trying to conceal his words.

"Aye, a wily one to boot, Marshal." He spoke in a heavy Scotch-English accent, introducing himself as Broc McKay. "Stromberg ... and them Drakes run this town. Quiet-like, but theyv's got a thumb on pert-near ever' thing, Marshal. You've gone crackers if yuh don't believe what I say. You've yer work cut out."

I thanked McKay and walked on to the jail house. Only a few shootin' irons hung on the walls now. One belonged to a miner I'd locked up for discharging his pistol in the street earlier that day.

"You're free to go, but I'll keep the gun until the twenty-four hours are up. Come back tomorrow about 3:30."

Begrudgingly he agreed, then walked out. Last I saw he was headed for one of the saloons.

Electricity & Magnets

Billy enjoyed takin' his schoolin' in the little room at the end of town with five other youngsters. Adding figures was his passion, and he enjoyed deciphering words from books and newspapers whenever he was idle. Most afternoons, when the town was quiet, I'd have Billy read a mite of this or that whilst sitting under a cottonwood near the creek. The primers he borrowed from the school were just right and he was comin' along well. Taught me a thing or two, things I'd not learned back yonder in the Nation.

Then we'd go up to the ridge shootin' cans. Billy wanted nothing more than to handle a pistol, and I could see he was a natural at drawing it out and taking careful aim. "Too many fellas git in a hurry," I told him. "Don't be rushin' to pull that trigger until you've leveled the gun barrel on your target."

By our fourth or fifth outing Billy could shoot nine out of ten tin cans I'd set up for him on a boulder up yonder on the ridge east of town. His confidence was growing, maybe a mite too fast.

That worried me.

Billy had accepted the loss of his parents more readily than one might expect. Had he grown numb to death? Or was he just a bit more resilient than other kids his age?

In many ways, Billy was becoming too much like me, adjusting to adversity, and figuring things out on his own. Meanwhile, was all this gun skill and preparation for adulthood takin' something away from his childhood days?

Vern Carlson owned the bank in Cactus Valley, a stoic man who kept to himself outside of his banking business. The few times we'd made brief acquaintances on the street, anxiety punctuated his demeanor.

Was Carlson a reliable barometer of things to come in town? Or was he just a nervous man? Gentlemen from back east seemed to be more uptight, it seemed. Still, I couldn't help wonder if Vern Carlson knew when trouble was in the wind. After all, the bank was a common target for thieves and renegades thought nothing of stealing what they could with the belief someone else's wealth was there for taking.

Vern kept shorter hours than I'd seen in other small towns, treating banking like a part-time enterprise. And now it was rumored he had over fifty pounds in gold, and another thirty in silver locked up in his safe. And with two town marshals dead inside of three months, Carlson was on edge.

Despite the growing population of Cactus Valley, the stageline came through just twice a week. Both were overnight stops to give the teams adequate rest. Temperatures on the desert were severe and the trail to Los Angeles often rough, sometimes with heavy loads of gold and silver from mines to the northeast in Nevada and Utah.

Overnight deposits were quietly made, then withdrawn, often before dawn, for transport the next day. The bank had been robbed three times in the six months it'd been operating in Cactus Valley.

Carlson's bank was a single-story building of sun-bleached clapboards in front, and reinforced stonework in the rear. A general store shared a common cement wall on one side and a blacksmith shop on the other side, directly across the street from Darla's Restaurant.

A creek ran behind the eatery and tumbled down a slope to the lower side of town where Vance Stromberg had erected three gambling saloons. The Hitching Post was the larger one, a stone's throw from the Cactus Hotel, run by Henry Drake.

The next morning rain settled the dust on the street and little activity was about. Mud in the streets was rare in these parts, and folks welcomed the fresh cool air, if only for a few hours. By noon there was little evidence of the downpour I'd walked through on my way to see Vern Carlson two hours earlier.

"Morning, Mr. Carlson." I closed the door behind me. His desk was in one rear corner and provided him a clear view of customers entering. A large black iron safe stood to his left against the stonework. I sat down across from Vern, who looked fresh and well dressed for the day. His desk was void of clutter other than a registry and a few sheets of unfinished paperwork.

Vern smiled and spoke softly in a hoarse tone. "Folks do appreciate the way you've stepped up," Marshal. "Glad to see someone take over the job."

"Well, I reckon it's a mite temporary, until they bring in a county sheriff or a federal marshal from out of town."

Vern Carlson nodded, then looked at me patiently. "What can I do for you, Mr. Llano?"

I took in a breath and glanced about the place. "Word has it you've got some gold and silver deposits waitin' to be transported out safely."

"Yessir. Some folks take their chances on the stage lines. Others pay an escort. But too many fellas lose their life, let alone their wealth trying it alone."

I nodded toward the safe. "If news of that gold is in the wind, and I didn't get it from you or the depositor, somebody's talkin' too much.

Carlson drew back an arm and pointed at a WANTED sign on the wall. A grainy photograph of Judd Reese advertised him as dangerous bank and stage robber.

"It's outlaws like him that make me nervous, Marshal. Until he's arrested ... or killed, anything might happen, right here in Cactus Valley.

"It's been a while, maybe three weeks since the last attempt was made on this bank. I can smell it in the air, Marshal."

"You mentioned the *last attempt*. What stopped 'em?"

"Noise. They was right noisy! Someone's dog started barking, which tipped off a couple of nearby residents. Old Broc McKay was the first to fire his shotgun into the air. That woke Sheriff Wade. So he come busting out of the jailhouse and nailed one of them. The other one, he fired back and killed Wade. But he rode out of here empty-handed. Nobody knows who it was, but folks think someone local is somehow involved ... tipping off a band of outlaws operating nearby."

"That someone you think is getting a share of the loot?"

"No doubt, Marshal."

I thought about that as I pulled out the makings. Smoking in silence whilst Carlson nervously filed away some papers, I got me some notions.

Suddenly I spoke again.

"So that's how the last sheriff was killed, huh. What about the one prior?"

Carlson nodded. "Almost the same way."

68

He gestured under the desk to reveal his firearms—a carbine rifle and two loaded Colts. "I don't want to shoot another man, Marshal, but things are looking more like I'll have to … just to stay alive."

I got to my feet and thanked Vern. "Say, where's the closest telegraph office from here?"

He drew in a breath and scratched his chin. "Reckon it's along the nearest railroad line, which is over a hundred miles north of here, Marshal."

"That's mighty far," I replied grimly. "If 'n we's ever to need additional help."

He shrugged and hunched back over his desk. "Stage line … or a fast horse is all we got."

"I see."

"Good day, Marshal. And by the way, you might talk with Keith Brender at the other end of town. He's a retired engineer who worked on the Union Pacific line. Helped manage the telegraph layout. Knows a sight about those things."

Feelings about me as marshal of Cactus Valley were mixed. Some folks in town smiled or greeted me on the streets, especially after seeing my willingness to stand up to Stromberg and firmly lay down the law. Others were skeptical about Indian folks mixing in with white man's business. And a few were plain ornery about having a "breed" living in their town.

I'd come out of the bank and stepped into the street when a gnarly voice rang out.

"Hey you, Injun Marshal! Why don't you go back to where you come from? Reckon we handle our own troubles round here."

His buddies broke out in laughter but I stepped around 'em with a tip of my hat, left handed like. They just watched me walk on by.

"What's the matter, Marshal. They say you is faster 'n a rooster in a dust storm!"

"That's right," I replied quietly. That rankled, but they weren't ready to see what I was made of.

When I knocked on Keith Brender's door his wife opened it and invited me inside. Her husband was hunched over an oak desk—a graying man with stooped shoulders and a sandy mustache. Mrs. Brender invited me to sit down in the parlor while she set the kettle to boil.

"Tea, Marshal?"

"Yes, ma'am." I smiled, then glanced over the room with an admiring eye. A grandfather clock ticked softly across from the stone fireplace and hearth. Furniture was sparse but finely crafted by skillful hands. Its dark polished finish reflected sunbeams pouring through two plate-glass windows. The Brenders were comfortable but lived in a humble manner. Soft spoken, each had been recipients of education and grace.

"What brings you by, Marshal?" Mr. Brender's voice was deep and resonant. His eyes gentle and attentive to me behind thick eye-glasses that sat low on his nose.

After some small talk on the weather and the town's recent growth, I asked him about the telegraph and its expansion west. He spoke slow and easy of the device's history, and how it would eventually be replaced with a "talking" device that could transmit human voices.

That's impossible, I thought. However, I said nothing of it aloud. Perhaps this man knew a sight about electricity. And he had his finger on the way of the future.

Time got away from us, as he showed me around his workbench, and spoke about men laying a trans-Atlantic telegraph line between Great Britain and New York City. That's when I asked Mr. Brender about batteries.

"You know, you're the *second* person who's asked me about batteries in this little town."

"Oh?" I replied with raised eyebrows. "Who was the first?"

"Vance Stromberg made inquiries when word had got around about my involvement in stringing telegraph lines along the new transcontinental railway. He was less interested in the telegraph, which struck me as odd … but was quite inquisitive about the *making* of electrical current."

Mrs. Brender was seated across the room, knitting. She looked up at me. "Mr. Llano, I don't know much about that man, Stromberg. But I get a strange feeling he's been up to something we have yet to see."

Keith Brender nodded. "The wife has a point, Marshal. Vance Stromberg and the Drake brothers have earned a keen reputation for fleecing good folks, and I wouldn't put it past them to harness electricity to expand their operations."

Drinking the tea in my cup, and listening to the Brenders talk, set me thinkin' right careful about Stromberg's gamblin' houses, and how them miners are losing their pay, particularly on the days they got paid for their work.

Brender went through the details of how one might construct a battery. It involved using unlike metals partially buried in the ground. "Copper is your positive side, and zinc is the negative side," he told me.

I asked him to tell me more about magnetism. "How does one harness electricity to create a magnetic field?"

Keith showed me a metal rod with wire coiled around it. "Engineers use a lot of these electric magnets to control pulses in telegraph communications."

I was fascinated, having heard of how pioneers of electricity were making new discoveries every day back east in the big cities. There was talk in the newspapers about inventing a light that was powered by electricity. Still, it seemed right impossible to common folks like me.

"So, how might someone like Vance Stromberg be using electricity to advance his gamblin' enterprises?" Knowing more about electric magnets, my imagination was running wild … but I wanted to hear what Brender thought.

His wife poured us another cup of tea and Keith lighted a corn-cobb pipe. His silver hair glistened in the sun light as he drew on the pipe and bit his lower lip. With mild hesitation, he laid it out in a series of questions, instead of answers.

"If you were running a gambling establishment, what would be your biggest concern?"

"Well … I'd want to be sure the house won more often than it lost."

"Indeed! If only to stay in business," he replied. "One employs a number of tricks with cards—it's been done for many years. But with a popular new device such as the roulette wheel and a steel marble, how must one assure himself of winning, particularly when the stakes are high?"

My thoughts went back to what I'd observed inside the Hitching Post. As it began to dawn on me, controlling the wheel or the marble suddenly became feasible. "A man might do something to manipulate where or when the marble falls or … doesn't fall onto the rotating wheel."

Brender nodded with satisfaction. He had led me to answers by fielding his own questions, in turn, spurring us to think this out together. I respected the man for he would have made a great school teacher.

A few minutes later, working at the dining room table, together we had sketched out the scheme we believed to be used by Stromberg! But it would be difficult to prove unless I could catch Vance Stromberg in the act. We even suspected there was more than one circuit to alter the course of the marble effectively.

I thanked the Brenders and let myself out. Returning to the jailhouse, I plopped down on my bunk situated near the cells in the back room. My thoughts drifted back to the power source. The battery. It would have to be connected to the circuit that controlled a magnet that was activated by electricity. Brender had laid out Stromberg's roulette wheel operation clearly.

I had work to do. I needed to discover how he was activating the magnets that controlled the marble's destiny on each spin of the wheel.

Meanwhile, my mind returned to the banker. He'd showed a sight of worry over them deposits inside his vault. Who in town would make an attempt on the bank? And when was the right time for a burglary to take place? A robbery was seemed likely since it was known Carlson kept a rifle and two pistols behind his desk. He'd gained a reputation for pulling the trigger more than once, wounding two men within a week of two holdups.

Would Judd Reese try a job on the bank after it closed, when folks in Cactus Valley were asleep? Or was he planning a daytime robbery?

Either way, I had me a way to keep Reese from getting his hands on that gold.

Billy Digs a Hole

About noon on Saturday I caught up to Billy crossin' the street after coming round the corner from behind the Hitching Post saloon. He was carrying a shovel with a busted blade.

"What's yuh got there, fella?"

"You know Ms. Peters, the old lady who lives out behind the alley? Well, yesterday she hired me to dig out a new latrine."

"Good to know you're git'n work, boy. You be sure to set aside some for harder times. No sense in livin' hand-to-mouth all yer life."

Billy smiled. "Yessir. Only, I busted her shovel diggin' around some metal I seen in the ground yesterday. Can't finish the job with a busted shovel." Billy raised up the blade, all twisted and comin' loose from its handle.

"Don't pay it no mind. I seen some right decent implements in that little shed behind the jail. Go borrow yourself a shovel out yonder."

Billy thanked me and disappeared around the corner of the jailhouse. The boy was becomin' right strong, and he kept good work ethics about him. And that pleased me.

I stopped over at Darla's for coffee to find several miners settin' down to a hot meal.

Saturdays, workin' folk was always looking to spend money in town.

"Howdy, fellas!" I offered cheerfully. One of them was the bearded man who'd bet five dollars on Stromberg's wheel a week back.

"You some kinda spin-golly, Marshal?" he asked eagerly.

"Don't reckon I know what you mean."

"I done a mite good last night on that there wheel! Some of the boys here did right well, too.

I raised an eyebrow. "On payday?"

"Yup! Stromberg seemed to be playing fair and square last night. Only he wasn't enjoying hisself! Not one bit."

"Glad to hear you made out."

From the conversation of these men, Stromberg's card games were as risky as ever, but I figured his roulette table was suddenly paying out at a normal rate instead of soaking every man jack who put down a bet. I finished my second cup and found my way out.

My rounds took me down the block where I saw Henry Drake enter the Hitching Post from the rear of the building. Wearing a scowl across his face, he ignored my neighborly wave. Everybody has their days.

I looped around and greeted folks in town coming out of the store and visiting. Before returning to the jailhouse I come along the boardwalk where a couple of ranch hands sat around lazily smoking and mumbling to each other. One fella was flicking beans at a dog who caught every one of 'em.

"Quite a catch, that dog is," I remarked.

"Like me at the Saturday night dance…"

"Reckon you'll need a good bath b'fore you can own up to such."

His pals chuckled and grinned from under their hats. "Like them greasers workin' out at the stables end of town."

"Might keep that talk under your hat. I hear one of them Perez boys done whooped the Pike boy for talkin' like that."

Nobody said anything.

Suddenly one of 'em looked up at me serious like. "You ain't doin' so bad here … and for a *breed*. I could git used to havin' things a mite peaceful here in town."

"Glad to hear it, fellas." I walked on.

Was I gettin' the hang of this marshalling business? I'd realized a good bit of it come by humoring folks and throwing out some perspective on life … not that I had a lot of it to offer. But my view point on simple respect could've been enough to make a difference.

*****

The Hitching Post was empty of patrons with only the hired bartender tidying up for the evening crowd. Stromberg was dozing in his office when Henry Drake strolled in through the back door and stepped into the dank office. He dropped his large frame into a black leather chair. Stromberg's eyes opened.

"What's this I hear about the house losing so much at the table last night?" Henry growled. "It's all over town the Hitching Post is a push-over!"

Stromberg bit off the end of his cigar and lighted it. Hesitating, he glanced over at Drake—an imposing man with cruel eyes that raised the hair on the back of any man's neck.

"It's that damn Injun marshal," Stromberg admitted. "That Llano Kid's got the whole town eatin' out of his hand like lapdogs, ever since he come in and played the wheel in front of them miners."

Henry Drake nodded. "I hear what you're saying … but we can't go on like this much longer. I got money invested in this joint, too. What do you plan to do about that roulette table … and that Injun marshal?"

The question hung in the smoky back office. Stromberg gazed at the end of his cigar and then knocked off the ashes. "As for that breed, I've been giving the matter some thought, Henry. I say we let him think he's a big man in town for a while longer. Then we'll have to do what has worked for us in the past. A marshal isn't worth a plug penny… dead."

"Alright, and what about that wheel?"

Stromberg shrugged. "I don't get it. The darn thing stopped playing out like it's supposed to. I've checked all the connections. Even called on old man Brender to take a look but he's down with rheumatism. Refuses to take on work these days."

Henry Drake stood up and turned toward the door. Shoving it open, he glanced back at Stromberg. "You better suspend games at that wheel, Vance. Shut her down until we can make repairs."

Stromberg nodded.

"And leave it to Reese and I to put that marshal out of business ... along with Munro's Bar M outfit."

*****

Just before sundown the following Saturday, the corral next to the livery was raked and ready for the Saturday night dance. The town held a shindig once a month

The torches were fueled up and burning. A wooden platform was in place for a five-piece band.

Folks were comin' in from all over the valley—more women than I figured were settled in these parts. Between the growing presence of ranchin' and the mining boon, the valley was becoming wealthy and more stable. The trouble makers were often forced to move on when enough good folks stayed around to carve out an honest living.

A large man with hard eyes rode into town on a tall horse, two men with him rode abreast. They drew up and swung down in front of Darla's restaurant. She appeared at the door and greeted them warmly. I watched them go inside about the time Billy showed up at my side.

He was grittin' his teeth and mighty sallow lookin', his hat pulled down over a shiny black eye. My hand went to his shoulder. "You have another run-in with that Pike boy?"

Billy bit his lip. "He says I'm yellow if I don't fight him."

I said nothing, unsure if anything I could say would do the boy right. Then he asked me about fighting.

"Teach me the kind a fella does with his hands."

"You mean boxin' ... or rass'lin'?"

"Both, I reckon."

Impressed with Billy's resolve, I smiled. For all the effort he'd put into shootin' a pistol ... and the state of mind he was in presently, I feared he'd be gunnin' for the school-yard bully.

"Well, Alright," I promised "We'll start on parrying an opponent's punches tomorrow. Meanwhile, I want you to put some effort t'ward making a friend out of that Pike boy, just the same."

Begrudgingly, Billy agreed.

Then, before he run off for supper a thought come to me. "Tell me more about that iron you dug up out there behind Ms. Peters' place."

Billy shrugged and kicked the dusty ground. "I'm sorry for—"

"No, Billy, that ain't what I had in mind." I gave a quick search of the street. "Why don't you show me right quick where yuh was diggin' that latrine for Mrs. Peters?"

We walked past the store on toward the Hitching Post, then cut down a side street where the ground was open with a pile of dirt near the alley. Billy pointed to the place, between Stromberg's gambling house and Ms. Peters' backyard.

My eyes went from the latrine's main hole, to a metal rod sticking up from the ground. A second rod was a good ten feet away from the first—both pounded into the earth with no more than two inches protruding from the surface. A copper cable was connected to the rod nearest the alley before diving into the ground and resurfacing near the other rod, its frayed ends lying in the dirt, no longer attached.

"This here the spot where you busted that shovel?"

He nodded.

"Alright, Billy. You done a good job digging that hole for Ms. Peters. But I want you to keep this damaged bit under your hat. Best I look in to it myself … and I'll see you tomorrow for that lesson."

Billy grinned and sauntered off for home. I set back on my haunches to do some studyin', concealed by prickly pear growing along the alley. I quickly unearthed more of the cable running between the two rods. This looked like what Keith Brender was describing the other day.

The makings of a battery?

Sounds of horse hooves and wagons broke my thoughts. I wanted to keep a tight rein on the dance. Some of the area's hot heads would be in town, and I'd tolerate no guns near the folks dancing.

Before leaving the alley I kicked dirt over the exposed rods and the broken cable. A few things about Stromberg's gambling operations were beginning to make sense, but I needed more evidence as to how he was fleecing folks in from the range and the mines.

The music began, and couples made their way onto the ground that had been raked and sprinkled with water. The air was still heavy but a light breeze began blowing about sundown. My hand-painted signs were nailed up, and posted real clear around the dance ground,

NO GUNS
WITHIN FIFTY FEET.

Despite all this, my rules against discharging firearms in town would likely be tested.

As it turned out, Gaylord Price was the large man I'd seen ride up just an hour earlier. When I introduced myself as the town's de-facto marshal, he raised an eyebrow at the notion of it happening here in Cactus Valley. But his eyes were friendly.

We shook hands and watched his ranch hands disappear into the crowd, grinning ear to ear at the ladyfolk.

"Them fellas you got there look mighty pleased to be to town."

"Aught to. They put in their hours."

It was a sight to see all the young ladies giggle amongst each other, watchin' all the young buck's lined up against the fence, combing their hair and adjusting their hats.

My words served well as an ice-breaker with Mr. Price and soon I knew he ranched on a small spread about three miles out of town. Told me how running cattle was catching on in the valley, what with all the laborers working in the mines. Once the mining operations slowed down, he figured the town would be settled in and populated enough to sustain ranching and other business ventures.

I asked him about other ranchers in the area. He stiffened a bit and looked me in the eye. "Can't say much good about 'em, to be right honest."

"Oh?"

I waited to hear more, as little news of the range outside of town ever reached me. "As you'd expect, water is a mite scarce in these parts. I got enough on my place, for a few hundred head … but the other outfits gambled on dry washes."

"So, they want some of what you got."

"Yep. Some rustlin' thrown in."

"Sound like a range war brewing?"

"Mebbe. Puts me smack in the middle."

"Where does W.C Munro fit in? I hear he runs some cattle east of town."

"His range borders mine for about a mile to the west. Good man, but right stubborn … and sore over having no access to the water comin' down off that mountain north of him. Leaves a burden on my shoulders to help out, but I can't swing it."

I suddenly recalled an afternoon of shooting practice with Billy. He was trying out his field glass when he seen several outcrops of lush green vegetation along a crevice coming down that mountain.

"Must be a half-dozen springs up the side of them slopes," I commented. "Too steep to run cattle up there, but it wouldn't be too much to capture that water. Water that could be shared by all."

Gaylord Price lit up a cigar and smoked in silence for several minutes. I could see he was a thinkin' man and preferred to say less than what he'd said already.

"I do appreciate your conversation," I told him. "If there's something I can do, just holler."

"Reckon I will," Price replied with a friendly nod. "One thing, Marshal. You best keep an eye on Henry Drake. He's got his mitts into plenty of business here in town, and it's him who controls that mountainside north of Munro's spread."

Now that was something to remember.

"I'll do that. Be seeing yuh."

I tipped my hat and went on about my rounds. There were plenty of well-grounded men here in attendance, which seemed to serve as a deterrent to anyone looking for trouble.

How long would it last, I did not know.

What Gaylord Price had said about Henry Drake nagged at me. Henry was a man of which I knew little, and just when it was a time to uncover a few stones, he come riding slow and easy into town.

A man was straddled across the back of Drake's horse. This drew a small crowd from the perimeter of spectators at the dance. When Drake pulled up, he sat his horse, silently, expectantly. I noted his eyes, cold and calm. When I come around Drake's horse to see who it was, somebody hollered, "That's Jess Culver! He's been workin' on the Bar M, not more than a couple weeks."

Henry Drake swung down and glared at me. "Marshal, what are you gonna do about this? There's a range war brewing out there!"

Ignoring his charged question, I wondered what business Drake had near Munro's spread, at this hour on a Saturday night.

"Where'd you find him, Henry?"

He described a place at the foot of the mountain, inside W.C. Munro's land. I studied his tone of voice and let him talk, figuring the less I spoke, the more I'd learn from his words, if not his body language.

"Marshal, don't it seem odd to you that this man was poking around not fifty yards from where my land intersects the Bar M? He was a long ways from any cattle Munro's running out there."

I turned to Drake. "I'll decide that after I have a look around. Meanwhile, would you take him over to the jailhouse? I want to have a look at the body."

The crowd broke and went back to where the dance was held. The mood had become a bit somber, and I heard no trouble from anyone that evening. I stopped at Darla's to ask about a town doctor. She told me there was no full-time doctor in Cactus Valley, but that her grandfather had some experience patching up soldiers during the War Between the States.

When George Whitney showed up at the jailhouse, I invited him inside and locked the door and drew the blinds.

He was a man in his sixties, with hunched shoulders and a cigarette dangling from his mouth.

George had a nervous twitch in his eyes, and smiled little.

The body of Jess lay across a table I'd cleared in the office. "George, I'd like your opinion on this shoulder wound."

"Somebody with a darn good rifle," he muttered while taking some measurements of the body. "And look at the angle of the shot, entering high on the shoulder, then exiting at the armpit. Too darn steep for a shot on that range land where you said he was found, unless …"

"Unless he was bent over shooting back at someone, or … the shot was fired from a hill or mountainside?"

Darla's grandfather nodded. "Like the mountain them folks is feuding over … but that isn't the bullet that killed him, Marshal."

"What?"

"It was this one." He ripped open the man's shirt and showed me a small hole that had entered the chest at close range. "I'd guess he was alive for several minutes after the first shot, seeing blood-soaked stains down the side of the shirt. But then, he died instantly of a second shot. Right here to the chest."

From the desk I drew out a tablet of paper and a pencil. "Would you be willing to write up a statement of what we're looking at here? I'll need some time after we bury the body before I can bring charges. And, George, don't mention this to anyone."

George agreed and handed me his printed account of the body. Then I had him leave through the back door where nobody could question him about the case. He returned the following day, driving a wagon behind his mule with a coffin for Jess on board.

Wasn't ten minutes after George left for the cemetery when Will Munro walks in looking mighty upset and beside himself.

"Marshal, you gotta do something!"

"What is it?"

"Folks is talking like I done killed Jess Culver. Accusing me of murder! That just ain't true, Marshal. Now why would a rancher go and shoot his own—"

"Alright, Mister Munro, you relax. I'll get some coffee on. You set and tell me what you heard … and who from."

He told me about how Henry Drake was dropping hints at the Hitching Post, claiming the Bar M was covering up a gold strike. That Munro was in the area when Jess was found near the mountain. How Munro didn't want anyone, including his own cowhands, to know about the gold he'd discovered.

The more I listened to Will's story, knowing what I did about the gunshot wounds … the more I believed Munro to be innocent. But I had to put it on the table.

"Is there gold on your land, Will?"

"Huh? Well, there may be some … After all, it's showin' up pert-near everywhere in these parts."

"Do your men know about any recent gold strikes? If so, who?"

"I doubt it, Marshal. With all the fence mending and searching for lost cows, there's no time to poke around in the rocks. Besides, that creek that used to run through my land is all dried up. Can't even water my stock, let alone pan for gold, Marshal."

That evening, after Will Munro left, I packed up Jess Culver's belongings to send on to his wife back in Kansas. He had a bowie knife, an empty wallet, and a broken watch chain. Somebody had looted the body.

But they'd missed the most valuable item!

Inside his boot was a folded paper. I glanced over its content and put it away for safe-keeping. The next day I would ride out to the Bar M and have a look around.

Blood on the Ground

It'd been a few days since I last took the roan out, so he was frisky and game for the trail. I decided to loop around the long way to the Bar M for the sake of giving him a good run.

I drew up at Will Munro's yard in front of a rambling house with a wide veranda. The corral was off to the left, the bunkhouse opposite. This provided a good view of whoever was coming from three different directions.

The cook was tossing out his dishwater when he seen me swing down.

"Howdy. I'm looking for Will Munro."

The cook glanced at the sun and back to me. "Reckon he and his outfit will be riding up any time for grub. Light and set. Coffee?"

"Couldn't be a better idea, partner."

He smiled. "You that new marshal they got in Cactus? Hear the town's quieted a mite."

I nodded, taking the cup he handed me. "Reckon it's what happens when good folks are willing to support law n order, when it's overdue. Can't take all the credit, myself."

"Well, folks is obliged to what yer doin in town, Marshal."

We talked a mite about range conditions, cattle, and the supply of water before Munro and his hands come riding up.

Over lunch I got directions from Will about where Henry Drake claimed to find Jess. "If you don't mind, I'd like to go out there alone," I told him. "Might ease suspicious minds if I handle things more official-like."

Will agreed. Besides, he had plenty of work to do on the range. "By the way, Marshal, we're missing a few head of white face cows. If you see any, let us know and I'll send one of the boys that way."

We parted, me riding north toward Drake's Mountain, and Munro south to the open range.

I let the roan amble lazily toward the mountain where the Bar M's range ended. An outcrop of basalt rock marked the vicinity where Jess Culver's body was picked up and brought into town by Henry Drake.

I swung down and left Smoke to feed off a patch of ocotillo that grew along the shallow bank of a dried wash. It took less than an hour before I spotted a trail of blood. Soon the evidence suggested he had moved from the spot where the first bullet entered his body to the place where he died, a distance of about seventy yards.

I retraced his steps from blood stains on the rocks with a constant eye on the mountainside. My intent was to reconstruct the scene of Culver's death, and determine the origin of the murderer's first shot. Had it been fired from a jagged ridge, which I estimated to be a hundred yards up the mountain? For behind that ridge, the rock became sheer, making a higher point at which a man could shoot from to be out of range for most rifles.

I decided, after some study, that a number of covered spots along the ridge were likely points of origin for the slug that was intended to kill Jess, but had failed. He had travelled by foot, then stopped to rest and perhaps that was when he made notes of what had happened. This suggested that he was losing a lot of blood and would die ... or believed his assailant would inevitably catch up to him and kill at close range.

Jess had managed to remove his boot and jam the note into it before slipping it back on his foot, apparently unseen by the man coming off the mountain. This suggested his cover was sufficient for but only the space of a minute or two.

Had the killer's trail down the mountain in pursuit of Jess kept him from keeping Jess in his sights? That notion helped me locate a couple different pathways the murderer had taken to finish the job.

Glancing over the spot where I believe Jess Culver died, I pulled out the map that come out of his boot and located the crevice in the rocks where Jess sighted gold. Sure enough, after a brief search, a long narrow vein could be seen in the shadows, and only at angle that was correct in the dapple light of late day.

I positioned a boulder in front of the entrance to the cove and scouted the mountainside where water trickled over stones. A confluence of springs flowed into a hole with a drop of some depth into what sounded like a well.

Back in town I returned the map to a seam beneath a floorboard in the office for safe keeping, then walked over to Darla's for supper. Lizzy was helping out today and brought me my usual, a beef sandwich with beans and potatoes on the side. I asked her about how she was getting on at the school.

Lizzy talked of her favorite stories, and how she was teaching herself to draw trees and horses in her extra time.

"That's real fine, young lady. We all need a hobby to keep busy … and out of trouble."

When I inquired about Billy she glared back at me with admonishment. "Can't figure him out, Mister Llano. All he cares about is fighting. Spends his afternoons punching at a sack of corn in the stables. Already busted two of 'em wide open."

I chuckled at that. "Reckon he's preparing to defend hisself from that Pike boy."

"Trouble started because Billy got some jobs that Remmy Pike wanted. Why can't them two shared the work in Cactus and git on just fine?"

I nodded at her wisdom. "You got a point there, Lizzy. You suggest that to Billy?"

"Tried. But he's got some revenge in him… ever since Remmy shoved him around in the school yard and called him yellow. I don't even think Remmy remembers that day, Marshal."

"Well, mebbe I'll talk to the boy. I reckon he's a little self-conscious."

Later that evening I rode out to the Bar M range, unannounced. The moon was up over the east horizon and provided just enough light to travel. I wanted to get a look at the site where Jess died in the evening, remembering that Drake had showed up with the body after dark. Other than the saloon traffic, town was quiet when I slipped out near ten o'clock.

I reached the foot of the mountain as the moon hung over me, illuminating the slope where I believed Drake had taken his shots at Jess. This gave me opportunity to see the mountainside from Jess Culver's perspective as he'd been trying to escape his pursuer.

Immediately I sensed something wrong. Something different about the area. The boulder I'd placed in front of the crevice where Jess had seen the gold vein was undisturbed.

So what was it?

I sniffed the air but found nothing unusual for that time of night. The sound of a polecat slinking along came to my ears …

Silence! That was the difference.

I realized it was the absence of the sound of water trickling off the rocky mountain shelf above me. No longer could I hear water spilling into the natural caldron on the lower slope. Earlier, water had been clearly audible, falling into the deep pool far below the surface. The absence of water spilling had allowed me to detect the sounds made by the most wary creatures of the night.

I climbed up to the stony mouth of the caldron and peered inside. Moonbeams cast a dim sliver of light on one then two ropes, dangling over the side. A heavy bead of water flowed over each rope, which explained the silencing of the water dropping into the pool. The remaining flow of water coming off the mountain hugged the rocky shaft wall.

I clutched one of the ropes and pulled. It resisted. Was some object tied to the other end? The second rope offered slightly less drag, though it too bore something of a load.

Quickly I reeled in the first until a burlap sack appeared in the moonlight at the rim of the caldron. Inside I found what I had suspected while pulling up the final length of rope.

Gold!

I let it back down, and rightly figured the other was of silver—both containing loot from Carlson's bank safe! Believing it would remain untouched for a few days, I let the ropes down. I saw no hurry to see it hauled off the mountain.

On my way out, I took a back trail that I'd not used but heard about from one of the Bar M hands at lunch the day before. Smoke took me into a shallow canyon said to emerge onto a narrow plain and over a ridge that overlooked town.

My mind wandered over this Bar M killing and its intersection with the bank job, which apparently occurred earlier this evening, quietly and uninterrupted.

Details of the scandal were coming together as I rounded a bend in grater darkness where the moon's light had all but failed to penetrate the canyon. It was with no pleasure that I found myself looking into the barrel of Judd Reese's six gun.

He had the drop on me!

"Well … fancy seeing you out here, Marshal."

"Beautiful night for a ride, I reckon." My remark was casual, hoping to buy time. "And how's that gun hand makin' out?"

Somehow in the darkness I sensed he was grinning with wicked eyes. "Well enough to kill a lawman." He paused. "Looks like you're too far from town for anyone to hear my shot … the one that will end it all for the Llano Kid!"

I shrugged my shoulders. "Reckon you got me dead to rights, Judd."

"It'll be my pleasure to see you die before another sunrise."

"Wouldn't deny a fellow a last cigarette, would yuh?" I slowly pulled out the makings.

His pistol wavered. "Don't see why not."

I let the match burn down as I spoke. "Heard someone hit the bank tonight. Too bad they beat you to it."

He let go an evil chuckled. "What's it matter to—"

"Ouch!" I yelped as the match burned my finger, and swept for my gun. My shot took Reese by surprise, spinning him around. He grabbed his shoulder, watching his gun fall to the ground. I covered him as I nudged the roan next to his horse and yanked his second pistol from its holster.

"Damn! Should a thought about that old trick," he growled.

After pulling off his boots, then tying his reins to the roan, I drew a piggin' string from my saddle and lashed his hands behind him. "Don't reckon you'll try anything now. Let's go, Reese. Yuh should've rode out of town when you had your chance. Now you got a barred room at the inn."

The Hearing

"Alright, hold your horses! I think we need to hear the marshal explain a few things." It was Darla speaking to the small crowd outside her diner. "After all, nobody else risked his neck to clean up this town like Mister Llano did."

Stan Webb got red in the face suddenly. "What's that supposed to mean?"

"Whatever you want it to mean," she replied curtly. Gaylord Price and WC Munro sat down, grinning at Stan. I stood up, intending to be as brief as possible.

"Folks, there's a simple explanation to this range war and the improprieties we've seen in Cactus Valley. We all know water is in short supply. That's part of living in a desert. But we also know it rains here and the desert has its own way of containing that water, as it does in rock formations and underground caverns. Mountains can hold vast reserves of water, releasing small trickles of it in the form of springs.

"But why would a man want to hold and protect his land where such springs exist, while he's unable to use the water for livestock or farming?

"However, a man could become very wealthy if he had both a grassy range and plenty of water. W.C. Munro has the perfect range at the foot of the mountain, but little water to keep a sizable number of cows. So, what is a logical thing to do?"

Mr. Price stood up and spoke loud enough for all to hear. "Buy him out!"

"Yes," I replied. "When he's willing to sell."

"I don't aim to sell," Munro put in. "Not until I'm busted and bankrupt."

"Precisely what someone with water has been waiting for." Turning my hat in my hands, I continued. "Yuh see, it's just a matter of time … unless our man can expedite the process somehow."

Drake appeared, flushed. "Now, Marshal there's no—"

"Oh? Maybe there *is* evidence." I was speaking to the group with intent for Henry Drake's ears. "Glad to see you could make the hearing, Henry. Please sit down."

"What's this all about, Llano Kid?" Drake demanded, refusing to use the title of Marshal.

"Simple. I'm making an arrest for the murder of Jess Culver, as well as conspiracy to illegally acquire the Bar M range."

Henry Drake eyed me with red hot fury. "You're crazy! You can't prove anything."

"I don't have to, Mister Drake. You'll do it for me. The proof is sitting in your hotel safe. You are in possession of a fake title to the Bar M, expecting to declare full ownership. You had it drawn up by Mitch Calhoun, a crooked lawyer in

Los Angeles, but it is of no use until one man could be eliminated."

"Who could that be, Marshal?" Darla's question was filled with bewilderment.

"Ma'am, that individual was next-of-kin to Will Munro, and had knowledge of gold on the edge of Munro's land. But then was killed when he'd been scouting the area. Shot from the mountainside by none other than Henry Drake."

Drake sprung to his feet and yanked out a tiny pistol from his vest pocket. But his foot caught the leg of his chair and his first shot fired into the front window of the restaurant. The second splintered wood shards at my feet.

As sudden as it began, the ordeal was over. Stanley Webb had Drake by the ear, against the wall as we saw the pistol clattering to the planks.

"Well, now. If that don't suggest guilt, I don't know what does. But folks here have a right to hear the whole story, including Henry Drake's scheme to cover up the fact there's a vast water supply inside that mountain, one that by law prohibits anyone from restricting its natural path into the valley.

"You may not know it, but out here in the desert there are laws against hording water if its natural flow moves through one's land and on to another's land."

"How'd you come by all this, Marshal?"

My eyes sparkled at Darla's question. "All them books in the marshal's office make for good reading on many a lonely night, ma'am."

I poured more coffee and sat back with a glance toward Stanley. No use in him standing there holding the walls up, so I tossed him a pair of handcuffs. He put the irons on Henry and I continued.

"You see, Henry Drake had cleverly diverted five of the springs on the mountain to flow into a deep cavern. To do this without detection, he used a pair of ropes on which the falling water silently ran down into a pool, a good sixty, seventy, mebbe a *hundred* feet below the surface."

I spoke of how I had discovered the pool the day I went out to look over the site where Drake had picked up the body. The sound of water spilling into the pool deep in the ground had been audible from the property line where Drake's land claim started.

"Yuh see, it was a day later, when I'd returned for the bullet casings, but this time there was no sound of the flowing water. So I hiked in closer and discovered someone had rigged up two ropes dangling into the shaft-like rock formation. Upon pulling them up several feet, the sound of water resumed.

"Yes, Mister Drake, a cunning plan to convince Will Munro there was too little water on the mountain to ever flow onto his land. And therefore eventually buy him out for pennies on the dollar."

Munro had remained silent, listening carefully to every detail. Now he raised a hand from where he sat near Darla.

"Marshal, it's gonna be mighty difficult to ever find that gold without Jess Culver around, I mean he took all that to the grave, including the man who killed him. Some folks in Cactus will still think I done it."

"On the contrary, Will! Before he died, Jess managed to scribble out the initials HD as the man who'd shot him from the mountainside before Henry could come down and finish the job. He even provided a clue about the location of that gold he'd discovered."

I pulled out the folded paper. "I found this in Jess's boot later that day. I've kept this secret so that I could build the case and prove Drake guilty with no distractions, Mister Munro. I've not only registered the claim in your name, but you're a free man."

"Well done, Marshal," Gaylord Price Reached out to shake my hand. "It all adds up perfectly, given the fact Henry Drake has been wanting to buy out the Bar M ... or run them out of business. A seamless plan to get prime cattle land, as well as inheriting a handsome gold claim."

Munro took the paper I handed him and glanced over its crude map. "I do thank yuh,

Marshal. It's good to see some closure to this range feudin'."

He shoved the paper into his shirt pocket and reached out a hand to Price. "No hard feelings?"

"None a-tall, sir." Price was glowing. "And when you're ready to bust up that dam upside the mountain, I'll help out."

The two ranchers stood up and started to leave along with the others who'd attended the hearing. But I wasn't finished. I turned to the banker who'd walked up and sat down.

"Mister Carlson, we need to return those bank deposits we got hidden at the jail."

Gaylord Price whirled around. "What are you jawin' about now, Marshal?"

"Well, I didn't say nothin' ... but Vern and I got a hunch old Judd would come after that gold you deposited for your cattle sales. So I dropped a few hints here and there in earshot of Henry Drake, and sure enough, Reese come around last night to break in and steal them dummy nuggets I had Billy and the Pike boy paint up. Yuh see, at night, when Judd busted into the bank and found the safe *accidentally* left open ajar, he failed to see he was packing out a bag full of painted river rocks."

Darla burst into laughter. "That's hilarious, Marshal!"

"It ain't all, ma'am. When I found them ropes in the water shaft on the mountain last night,

I pulled 'em up and found Judd Reese's fake loot. Then he come by me on the trail … and well, intending to put me six-feet under, he got hisself arrested instead. Got him over at the jail now, where Henry can join him."

After locking up Henry Drake I stepped out onto the jailhouse porch and announced that I had business over at Stromberg's Hitching Post, and would they join me.

Darla looked at me sharply. "What business do any of us have at that lowdown drinking establishment, Marshal? What's gotten into you?"

I grinned back at her and the others. "Trust me on this one, ma'am. I think y'all will find this next act even better!"

Price and Munro raised eyebrows and shrugged. "What do we have to lose?"

When the lot of us walked into the Hitching Post, the joint was empty, other than a couple miners playing cards at a table in the corner. Despite the stale odors of spilled liquor and man sweat, it was pleasant to get out of the dense heat that hung over the street. The bartender glanced at us and set a bottle up on the bar.

"Hello, Marshal. The boss says this one's on the house."

"Oh, we're not here for pleasure, Mel. No sir," I drawled. "We got us some o-ffi-shul business here with Mister Vance Stromberg, Owner and Proprietor." I let that drawl I'd acquired in Texas melt over my words, for effect—a sort of lazy lawman's way of easing into breakin' some bad news on somebody who's had it coming for a long time.

Having overheard a few of my words, Vance Stromberg slinked into the room from some back office. His eyes glinted toward the others and then me. The smile on his lips did not exist in his eyes.

"What's your game today, Marshal?"

"Funny you should ask that question, Vance … because folks in Cactus Valley have been wondering what *your* game is for some time."

I motioned to Darla and Gaylord Price to sit down. Old man Webb took a seat opposite, along with Willian Munro, who spoke right up:

"I've a few bones to pick with the Hitching Post's owner, Marshal, on account of my ranch hands getting fleeced whenever they come into town to play that durned wheel."

"Well, I reckon this little meeting will cover some gambling-related improprieties," I replied.

First thing, I had the bartender put away that bottle of whiskey and pour us all water since I had sobering business at the Hitching Post.

Their eyes settled on me patiently.

"Folks of Cactus Valley are right curious about how that new-fangled roulette wheel works,

Mister Stromberg. Would you do the honor of a demonstration?"

His lips thinned as contempt for me paled his large jowls. But he was quick to compose himself, looking for a last chance to legitimize his operation.

Gaylord Price looked around the room with interest. "I've heard of these newfangled dee-vices, Marshal. But I never figured on betting hard-earned money on one. Prefer a fair hand of poker, myself."

"That's fine and dandy," I said. "Today yuh git to see how one operates, fair and square."

"Stromberg glared at me. "That roulette wheel is closed for repairs, Marshal."

"Well," I spoke to the others, intending it more for Stromberg. "that leaves me to demonstrate a few things on my own." I stood up and we walked over to the table where the wheel sat under a leather cover.

Suddenly Vance swung around the bar and faced me square.

"Alright, Marshal. But I think you're wasting my time ... and their time. Nor can you prove anything against me, if that's what you're intending."

"Did I suggest that?" My reply was trite. "I simply asked you to show us how this wheel works, that is ... when your patrons are gathered round the table during business hours."

Stromberg grumbled under his breath and pulled the cover off the wheel. I reached over and set a few chips on various numbers, and then stacked several on the felts indicating anything red.

"Okay, Vance, give 'er a spin, and let go that marble like you do when the joint's full of gamblers."

He shot me a sly look through his good eye as he released the steel marble. We all watched the marble round the wheel and drop into the slot labeled *13*.

"You can see that sometimes you win and sometimes you lose, depending on where the marble falls on the wheel," I explained. "Nothing dishonest about that. But what if the house wanted to avoid a big win on a particular number, stacked with chips?"

Darla leaned on the table and glanced at Stromberg, then back to me. "Why ... you'd have to figure out a way to make that marble fall on a small bet."

"Huh! Or, no bets at all," Mr. Munro added sharply. "That's what I hear from my cowhands. Then one of them Drakes or some other friend of the house strolls in, bets, and walks out with a hundred dollars ... or more!"

Vance Stromberg was beside himself. "That's a lie!"

"Is it, Vance?" Gaylord Price spoke evenly.

Stromberg sighed. "I don't know what the marshal's talking about. This here is a respectable business. Marshal saw it for himself last time he was in here. I got work to do. Good day, folks!"

"Now, I'm sure the jury would look upon Mister Stromberg in a better light if he were to cooperate."

Seeing that Vance Stromberg was ready to bust a gut, the chance of him drawing a gun lingered on my mind. Though I doubted he was packing his Derringer because he always wore it at sundown. Besides, he was no gun fighter, having hired out others to do his dirty work. Still, I believed him to be a dangerous man when he was cornered.

"You can't prove nothing against me!" he growled.

Gaylord Price shook his head at Stromberg. "If it looks like a dog and it barks ... it's a dog!"

He said nothing to that, so I let it hang before stepping back from the table. "Okay, let's find the smokin' gun," I chuckled. "Take a good look along the table's finished edge. Do you see anything unusual?"

Stromberg looked on casually, hoping nobody would find what he knew was there.

"Right here, Llano. Take a look at this!" Darla was the first to notice a small circular cut-a-way flush in the side of the table.

By now the two poker players at the table in the corner had put their cards down and wandered over, gazing at the spot Darla was pointing at. One of 'em shot me a sobering look.

"What are you gittin' at, Marshal?"

"I'm saying this is a controlled wheel."

Suddenly guilt was painted all over Stromberg's crimson face. He was a powder keg ready to explode, but he held his fuse.

"That's just *one* of his secret buttons," I told them with a wry grin.

Darla gazed back at me. "You mean there are more?"

"He's got *three* buttons to control where the marble settles on the wheel. That is, only when he's got a source of electricity."

"Electricity? You mean that stuff they use to send a telegraph message?"

I nodded. "That's right, Mister Webb. This shady operation only works when there's electricity to power the magnets!"

"I've read about them piles they made out of metals over in Europe," Gaylord Price added. "I believe they call it a *battery*."

I looked at Stromberg, intent on keeping him involved in the hearing leading up to his own conviction.

"That sound right, Vance?"

Stromberg only grunted, his words barely intelligible. "Why don't you prove it, Marshal?"

"Well now, I was afraid you'd never ask."

Stromberg didn't know that I knew the table hadn't been working the way it was supposed to, and that the house had suspended roulette games most evenings since the day Billy had busted the cable off the metal rod in the alley. And I said as much, drawing some interested looks from the group, the biggest one coming from Stromberg!

"Yuh see, Mister Stromberg, I took it upon myself to make sure your *battery* was in working order. In fact, I repaired that cable a couple days back. Saying nothing of it, I guess you missed out on some business."

Darla gazed up at me, still pointing at the button on the side of the table.

"Push on it!" I told her.

She did, and we heard a soft click on the rim of the roulette wheel. A tiny pin was protruding from the banked turn where the marble would be redirected onto the wheel.

We found the other two buttons underneath the table, all within finger's reach of the roulette wheel operator. I had Gaylord Price spin the wheel, and Darla released the steel marble. All eyes were on that little steel marble when I seen Vance from the corner of my eye retreat toward the bar where he kept a pistol.

"You ought not try it," I said quietly. "I believe Stan's got you covered with that Walker Colt he's always carryin' around."

Ole Vance was lookin' mighty sick about then. He sat down like a defeated dog. Stan shot me one of them inquisitive looks.

"How'd you know I carried this here Colt, Marshal?"

"It's my job to know them things, Mister. Webb."

He grinned back at me, then commenced to covering Vance Stromberg with one eye whilst he watched the marble with the other eye.

It was a sight to see!

"You hold that button down with your finger, Mister Munro, and you'll see that *nothing* on black will win."

Sure enough, the marble dropped onto a RED number. We repeated the demonstration several times, never seeing a black number come up on the wheel, as long as Will held down that button. Then we did the same with a second button, barring any red numbers from coming up.

"I think we've seen enough, Marshal." Darla shook her head in disgust.

I ordered Mel to close up the joint until we had us a little talk about him taking over its operations, for I knew Mel was an honest man trying to make a fair living.

"Alright, Mister Stromberg, your numbers are played out. I arrest you for running a rigged casino operation with intent to deceive patrons, based on the evidence disclosed therein."

Darla gave me a look like I just stepped out of the grave. "Oh, now didn't that sound like real lawyer talk, Marshal?"

"Some of them words come right out of the books I'd been reading in the jailhouse, ma'am."

We'd had us a good laugh and just gotten to the front door when Billy come down the street tossing a ball with the Pike boy.

I gestured to Gaylord Price. "Have Billy show you that earth battery out back. Take a good look at it, then have them two boys dig it up … and tell 'em Mister Stromberg will pay them for their work."

Price and the others chuckled. Stan Webb's eyes sparkled. "Now there's a notion I like. The town crook can start paying back his community by providing jobs for our young lads."

End

The Llano Kid is gonna be right honored to know you wrote a review of his story on Amazon, and shared this book with a friend!

Author's Notes

Cactus Valley is a fictional town in the northern vicinity of the Mojave Desert

By the mid 1870s gold and silver was still found in southern California, though in smaller quantities.

While it was unheard of to see an Indian marshal in a white settlement, those with at least half their blood lines from white stock were occasionally accepted as viable citizens.

Some of America's most respected bounty hunters and soldiers were men of color, particularly African American.

The advancement of harnessing electricity was taking hold in the 1870s with the introduction of the light bulb, but little of it was realized in rural America until later.

Controlling a roulette wheel became a concern in later years but rarely at the level of accurate manipulation as the one depicted in this story.

Earth battery technology of the late 18th century had migrated from Europe. Power generation stations soon made electric current available for lighting and locomotion, in large urban centers

such as New York City. Rural areas waited
another fifty years.

Made in the USA
Middletown, DE
29 July 2022

70190541R00068